TASK FORCE (
DANI'S GOT A GUN

The Men of Five-0 #4

Dixie Lynn Dwyer

LOVEXTREME FOREVER

Siren Publishing, Inc.
www.SirenPublishing.com

A SIREN PUBLISHING BOOK
IMPRINT: LoveXtreme Forever

TASK FORCE ONE: DANI'S GOT A GUN
Copyright © 2012 by Dixie Lynn Dwyer

ISBN: 978-1-62242-285-2

First Printing: December 2012

Cover design by Les Byerley
All art and logo copyright © 2012 by Siren Publishing, Inc.

Printed in the U.S.A.

PUBLISHER
Siren Publishing, Inc.
www.SirenPublishing.com

TASK FORCE ONE: DANI'S GOT A GUN

The Men of Five-0 #4

DIXIE LYNN DWYER
Copyright © 2012

Chapter 1

Daniella "Dani" Lynch was recently assigned to a murder investigation involving a potential serial killer. One look at the previous ten cases and it didn't take her five years as a detective to figure out they were in fact after a serial killer. A very gruesome one, if you asked her. Every crime scene contained massive amounts of blood, destructive surroundings, and multiple bodies. The first few crime scenes contained single bodies. To her, it seemed their killer was getting more confident, cocky, and hopefully sloppy so she could catch him or her.

She had gotten a potential lead after questioning some local delivery guys who had practically interrupted one of the murders. They got a look at what they thought to be a very large, oddly shaped person who from their perspective, appeared to be wearing a mask of some sort and also had furry legs. That didn't sit right with her at all. The other detectives hadn't found any evidence left behind in regards to synthetic fur, plastic, material or anything indicating that a person in a costume was present at the scene. But in her experience, many odd things occur at a crime scene, and she wasn't taking the men's description lightly. Perhaps their killer dressed in costume to remain unidentifiable? She wasn't certain, but the killer was last seen around a warehouse across the parking lot from where she'd parked her Mustang. It wasn't that she expected the killer to be lingering around only a few blocks from his last killing spree, but she thought she would get a vibe for the area. Maybe something that could help her to track it down or gain a better understanding of the killer's profile. She got out, checked her weapon, and headed toward the building. That was when she heard the screams and noises coming from somewhere in the large warehouse. She called it into the department as the alarms began to blare. She reached for the door, finding it unlocked, and was surprised that anyone would be around this time of night. Her gut clenched and she had a feeling that something bad was about to happen. Someone was in trouble.

Dani slowly reached under the handle of her Glock to click the button on the flashlight. It was freaking dark in the warehouse and the blaring siren from the alarm wasn't helping her already splitting headache. She held her finger against the trigger. If anything moved, it was dead. She sniffed the air as the slight smell of smoke filtered through the building. This was the asshole's MO. Kill whomever it wanted to kill then burn the evidence. Not tonight. Not with her hot on its trail and ready to put this case to an end and bring justice to ten devastated families.

Her luck in catching this asshole seemed to be getting better. Dani had just so happened to be in the right area at the right time when the call from dispatch came through. She'd listened to the radio dispatch knowing that if the surrounding neighbors heard the screams, then it was pretty bad. The alarm sirens must be drowning out the screams from where she stood in the building. Dani wasn't sure if it was the dispatcher's description from a caller about hearing screams or the location of the warehouse. Either way, it brought her here, and the killer was still in the vicinity.

She had heard a series of cries upon entering the building. She followed the direction she felt they came from until the sirens blared louder, indicating precisely where they were triggered to go off. She knew from investigating the other cases that this was the killer's regular routine. The fact that he set fire to his victims after killing them told her that he was hiding something. But what? Rape, sodomy, his fingerprints and DNA? Or perhaps some remnants of his hairy costume the guys described. She snorted lightly. Anything was possible and her mind was in detective mode.

The victims were mostly female. She needed answers. As a detective, the unanswered questions drove her to investigate and capture the one responsible.

It's so fucking dark in here. I hate this feeling.

Slowly she took a few steps, something sticky clung to the soles of her black boots. She didn't like the instant uneasy feeling she had. She didn't have a weak stomach. There was no room for one as a homicide investigator. Dead bodies, murder, suicide were all daily occurrences and exactly what her job was all about. She was a murder cop and damn good at solving crimes. She lifted her foot again and sensed that whatever she was stepping on was gooey. It was thick, and as she sniffed the air again, afraid to move the flashlight down to the floor in case the killer was still somewhere close by, she absorbed the sting of something metallic. She could almost taste it on her tongue.

A feeling inside of her suddenly came alive. It wasn't a sensation she was familiar with. It almost made her forget where she was and that a killer hid in the vicinity around her.

She heard a gurgling sound and moved the flashlight slightly to the right. Her heart pounded inside of her chest. The last breaths of life. A victim, staring at her pleading for help. She raised her hand as if indicating that she would indeed help the dying woman, but everything Dani learned on the streets and from investigating murders told her that it was too late.

"Help is on the way," she whispered, and she noticed the woman's eyes change. They sparkled as they held Dani's gaze. Again something deep within her pulled forward and seemed to touch the woman in front of her. The woman's eyes widened as if she, too, sensed the strong feelings Dani had inside. Dani knew it wasn't possible, but her gut tried to battle with her realistic mind. Was the sensation Dani had a coping mechanism as she faced death while on the hunt? She wasn't certain.

"They're on their way. Just hold on for me," Dani whispered and the woman smiled, bowing her head to Dani. When she opened her eyes, they were glowing yellow.

Dani gasped as she took a step back. What the hell? How did she do that?

The fucking alarm still roared and the stench coming from the floor was making her belly quiver. She looked down, shone the flashlight across the floor where she stepped and she gasped in shock. It was a pool of blood. There were bodies everywhere. *Holy fuck!*

She heard the deep growl and things banging around in the distance. Swinging her head in that direction and then her body, she remained holding her Glock and pointing it in the same direction. Her finger was steady despite the turmoil she felt and the multitude of emotions of the scene.

She turned the flashlight, pointed her gun, and holy fuck, what in the world?

Some hairy, enormous, wolflike creature standing on two feet held a man by his throat. The lifeless body swung back and forth as the wolf shook it like a rag doll.

"Stop! Police!" she yelled.

She was beyond scared. What the hell was that thing?

The way it looked toward her as if it understood English made her nearly take a step back. She held a gun. What the hell did it have to fight her with, the claws and sharp teeth? She realized rather quickly that she wasn't willing to chance negotiating. Not against that.

It was some sort of massive animal or something. That was no costume but the real thing. The teeth were ferocious and huge. It stared right at her with dark black eyes that reached her soul.

She had a feeling it wasn't human at all when suddenly the fire alarms began to blare even louder than the alarm system, indicating that the fire was moving in closer to the floor she was on. The smoke thickened around her, blocking her view. It was so freaky and almost magical how he disappeared from her vision. That sensation she hadn't recognized earlier reemerged. She felt it deeply and acknowledged it. Her defenses were up, her need to protect and restore life invaded every other thought and even her law enforcement training. She knew with all her being that this killer was not like any other.

It roared again, and she could have sworn that it headed toward her. The sound of its roar vibrated against every part of her body, making her shake. But she fought to remain somewhat calm as she gripped the Glock tighter and slightly began to pull the trigger. If it came at her, she was going to kill it. As soon as she had a good shot, she was taking it. She turned right, felt the brush of air and its presence too close for comfort.

"Show yourself, asshole! I dare you!" Dani yelled as she gripped the Glock with both hands. Now her palm was under the handle as extra support. Her insides may be shaking, but her arms were steady, her finger on the trigger ready to apply the right pressure necessary to discharge her weapon. Keeping a steady hand took years of experience and dozens of incidents like this as a cop on the streets. But something told her that this case was different. This thing was not like any killer she hunted before.

It came back again, this time it brushed by her ever so slightly and she caught a glimpse of its face, not quite fully wolf but something else. Human?

It was messing with her. It was confident that it couldn't be caught, and it looked at her as if she were nothing but another victim. *Fuck that.*

She felt the challenge, the need to prove herself capable of its challenge if that was its intention. A moment later she felt it whiz by her again. She hadn't a chance in hell to shoot. It was that quick, that good.

It roared a loud, ferocious roar, and she sensed it heading straight toward her this time. It was done playing games. Dani felt that sensation again deep inside of her. It was powerful and made her react more quickly than she thought possible.

She turned just as it approached, mouth wide, enormous teeth prepared to bite into her flesh and rip her apart like the others.

She pulled the trigger. One, two, three shots rang out and echoed in the distance. She twirled around, looking for it. "Where the fuck did you go?" she screamed, her voice cracking as she circled around too fast, making herself feel dizzy. Her mind shouted numerous things. *You got it. It has to be injured or dead. What huge fucking teeth it had. Stop shaking. Focus, Dani, focus.*

She began to cough. The smoke was getting worse. She was too late. That thing was responsible. That thing set the fires but how? It wasn't human. It was some wild-looking beast.

She knew she had to head back down to safety, but she wanted to catch the killer. She was so close when suddenly the ferocious beast leaped across her path. She tried shooting again, but it knocked right into her. The hit sent her flying a few feet across the concrete floor and over the thick blood her boots had stuck to only moments ago.

Somehow she held on to her gun, and as she shifted left then right, she heard the glass from the window shatter. It leaped right through and disappeared into the night.

* * * *

"You been drinking or something, Detective?" the sergeant asked her as she tried to wipe the blood off of her neck and arms.

"No, sir," she stated, trying to watch her tone and her attitude. Sergeant Ass Wipe would never change. He could never be a detective like she was. He was lazy and hadn't an instinctive gene in his body.

"Wolves bigger than men and blood-soaked floors?" he teased as a few other officers stared at her.

Screw them and their chauvinistic attitudes. She earned her detective rank and not from spreading her legs to any brass either.

"Look at my clothes. I took a fucking bath in it. Why do you think forensics took samples of evidence from me? You know what, I don't need to have this conversation with you." She stood up, trying her hardest to ignore the burning sensation on her shoulder.

She needed a change of clothes, a nice, hot shower, and perhaps a beer. This killer was making her crazy. She wanted to catch him badly, and tonight she blew her chance.

"The commander wants to see you," Sergeant Ass Wipe yelled to her.

"Tomorrow he can. I'm outta here." She walked away from the police cars and to her own Mustang GT parked behind a large tree in the darkness. She hid it there earlier in the night.

She walked around toward the trunk and unlocked it. Pulling out a black duffle bag, she grabbed a new T-shirt. A quick glance around and she quickly removed the bloody one and replaced it with a clean one.

That burning sensation hit her shoulder again, and the hairs on the back of her neck stood up. She turned around slowly, trying to take in any movement or bodies hiding between the trees.

She still wasn't sure of the other sensation that had engulfed her back in the warehouse. It was something she had never experienced before. She had connected with that victim during their final moments before death. She almost felt as if she helped her to relax before she died. Dani shook her head. She was losing it. She needed sleep, and she needed to catch this piece of shit.

She was a street cop for years in New York City. She learned fast
to always be aware of her surroundings and never turn her back on the
enemy. Her gut instinct saved her more than a handful of times.

Someone or something was watching her.

She couldn't help the uncomfortable feeling she had. It was
almost like a fight-or-flight instinct. She needed to run. Exercise,
especially running, helped to calm her mind and bring her peace, but
tonight it would only make her antsy.

She closed the trunk, and there by the driver-side door was a very
tall, distinguished-looking man staring at her. She wondered if he had
seen her strip her shirt off and she was grateful for the sports bra that
remained in place and the very bad lighting.

"Who are you?" she asked as she stood in her position a few feet
away.

* * * *

Zespian Fagan took in the sight of the gorgeous young woman
before him. When he'd identified himself as Special Investigations
Commander to the sergeant in charge of the current crime scene, he
was directed to go talk with the witness. Making his way through the
crowd of human law enforcement, he noticed a few other weres
amongst those investigating, and he was pleased. They would know
what to do. They would ensure that the investigation didn't leave any
questions or concerns to the human police. This was a job for
werewolves. The firefighters had entered and soaked down the
majority of the blood with their water hoses. That would help, too.

"Yes, miss, my name is Commander Zespian Fagan." He reached
out his hand and she looked at him suspiciously. She wasn't fearful.
He could sense her emotions, and if anything, she seemed on the
defensive and ready for a fight.

"It's Detective Lynch, Commander Fagan," she replied with
attitude but reached to shake his offered hand.

"Pleasure to meet you, Detective. I understand that you're a witness to tonight's events?"

"I'm not a witness. I was trying to catch the killer," she stated as she opened her car door and leaned over the top frame of it. "You said Commander Fagan. Commander of what?" she asked, looking him over.

She was tough, for a human.

"Commander of Special Investigations."

She raised her eyebrows. It seemed Detective Lynch knew of the unit.

"And what brings you around here, Commander? I mean usually your associates in the Special Investigations Unit don't visit crime scenes. Is this connected to something you're working on?"

He looked her over, unsure why he had even come over here to meet her face-to-face in the first place, but there was something interesting about her scent. It wasn't an attraction or sexual pull but a familiarity. He needed to find out more about her and her bloodline, her family history. Something inside him pulled to full attention. It was a part of him he never talked about or revealed. Why did this woman remind him of this well-hidden part of himself? He would need help to investigate her. The department computer he'd accessed through his phone didn't turn up shit.

"This is an interesting enough case, don't you think, Detective?" he asked her, and she looked pissed off. She was obsessed with this case. He knew it, could tell right away how possessive she was and how determined she was to find the killer. Considering she was human, that might cause a bit of a problem.

"The case is mine, Commander. I mean no disrespect, but I've been busting my rear trying to find this thing."

"This thing?" he asked.

She shook her head and lowered her eyes.

What exactly had she seen? The rogue wolf had shown its face to a human? He must have thought he would kill her but she escaped.

"Forget it. I'm tired and I've been up all night. I'm really not in the mood." She glanced at her watch. He could smell the metallic scent of blood on her body and saw the stains on her wrists. That would irritate a wolf with such keen senses but not a human. She would wash it off in the shower and be done.

He needed to know what she saw and why the beast released her.

"Before you go, Detective, tell me what you saw," he stated firmly. She looked up from the forearm she rested her chin on and stared at him a moment.

"I didn't see shit."

With that she got into her sports car, closed the door, and took off.

Zespian pulled out his cell as he watched her black Mustang. This was a job for the family. He needed his nephews' help.

"Fagan, I have a potential situation. You and your brothers need to meet me, now."

He closed up his cell and glanced around the area. His lupine senses were in overdrive. It was near. It was still in the vicinity, watching. He looked around, using his wolf night vision to see through the trees. Detective Lynch's Mustang had just pulled past the police perimeter set up to secure the crime scene. The left blinker indicated she was turning onto Price Street. There, there in the shadow of darkness it stood in the form of a man.

Zespian wanted to take off after it. He couldn't see clearly, just the image of a male, its face turned sideways, giving him the profile of something caught between wolf and man, almost a half shift. That was possible but took a well-trained wolf to do. He was more than wolf and man. But its merciless killing spree could potentially cause major problems. This thing wasn't thinking clearly. It was crazy or some kind of hybrid. Zespian wasn't certain. It was speculation at this point. It was a freak of the supernatural world that needed to be caught and killed. He hurried toward his car as the thing headed in the same direction as the detective.

Chapter 2

"We've got another one," Zespian informed his five nephews as they gathered around the living room in the main headquarters. It was a secret room, set up by a government affiliate for their particular organization. The Special Investigations Unit was an elite force of were packs assigned to cases that threatened to exploit or expose the were community to the humans. It had been in existence for many generations and used the protection of the Secret Order of the Brothers of Were when necessary. Zespian had the feeling that his nephews, Van, Miele, Randolph, Baher, and Bently, were perfect for this particular operation. Zespian needed his closest family members involved with this, especially if this woman turned out to be connected to Zespian in some way. Van and his brothers came to mind immediately after sensing some sort of familiarity to Detective Lynch. Plus, Zespian's secret needed to remain that—a secret, or his family could suffer from the results of a decision he'd made over a century ago. Through his gut instincts and family heritage, he had always been able to sense when someone was of evil or of good. He could also sense when there was a bond or connection of sorts. He knew that many paths crossed during his thousand years of life and that this ability had helped to achieve success in his position and helped to ensure the sanctity of the were race. Tonight was no different. In fact, tonight seemed to have the undertone of power, importance, and trouble. Detective Lynch needed protection. He had followed her to her apartment, and the wolf had disappeared. It was as if the monster only wanted to know where she resided. It was cunning, intelligent, and had evaded capture for months now. The department needed help.

He saw his nephews enter the room one at a time. They were extra large men, muscle-bound and exuding bad-ass attitudes that scared people and wolves shitless. This monster, out-of-control killer would be somewhat of a challenge for them. It was sneaky and intelligent, but they were the best he had. Their success in Ireland and in Mexico more recently proved their abilities. They were a hell of a team.

* * * *

"Hello, uncle." Van bowed his head then thrust his large hand forward to shake Zespian's. Zespian smiled, and then pulled Van into a bear hug. It backfired on him as Van picked him up and squeezed back with half his strength, causing Zespian to lose his breath.

"Son of a bitch, Van. You're going to squeeze the life outta me." Van chuckled then lowered his uncle.

"Well, you challenged first," Van replied then winked, his green eyes sparkling with mischief.

Zespian shook his head as he fixed his shirt.

"So what's the deal?" Miele, Van's brother, asked. He was the antsy one, always ready to do the next thing on the agenda. He had light brown hair and hazel eyes like his brother Baher.

"Well, come gather around. This may take some time to go over."

"That bad, Zespian?" Bently, the most easygoing of the brothers asked.

"Afraid so. I believe we've got another rogue wolf on our hands and loose in the city," Zespian informed them. A series of annoyed growls and curses whispered through the room.

"Who the hell is it?" Van asked.

"Not certain. That's why I called you guys in. It seems to be a bit different than the others."

"Different how so?" Baher asked this time. He was the most stubborn of the men. Their brother Randolph spoke the least and still remained silent as he stood by the doorway leaning against the doorframe. His facial expression alone was beyond intimidation. Zespian glanced at each of them. Sporting tattoos, all dressed in black and each over six feet tall, they indeed were the epitome of Alpha wolf.

He began to tell them about the occurrences over the last month and about what he witnessed tonight and his theory about a hybrid.

"Damn," Bently replied to the information.

"I guess we'll cut in now and take this case over? Did you inform the brass?" Van asked.

Zespian shook his head.

"I don't want to do that just yet. There's a detective working the case and—" Before Zespian could finish his sentence, his cell phone rang. By the tune of the ring, he knew it was important. He answered it, gave a few one-word responses, then covered the receiver.

"There's a file there on the table. That's the name of the detective on that sticky note, an address, and more info on the victims killed thus far. I need to take this call and it's going to be a while. I call you later and explain." Zespian told them.

"We'll take care of it." Van reached for the file.

Their uncle headed out of the room.

* * * *

"So what do you think?" Bently asked Van as he looked over his shoulder at the file.

"You and Miele can question the detective. It's a guy by the name of Dani Lynch. Randolph, Baher, and I will try to get a scent or some indication of a lead off the crime scene. The cops should have wrapped up hours ago." Van glanced at his watch. His brothers nodded, and Bently and Miele grabbed the address of the detective and headed out.

* * * *

Dani was achy from the attack last night. Her ribs were sore from where that monster banged into her, but there was no bruising or discoloration. The extra few pounds she couldn't shed must have provided some cushioning. She pulled on her black pants then clasped the button over the slight swell of her belly. Yeah, she could stand to lose a good five pounds or so. Turning sideways, she looked at her ass. It may be big, but it looked really good in these black pants. Her boobs weren't too bad either. The extra weight made them more than a handful and from the compliments of past lovers, she was not lacking there either. *Past lovers? Shit, why the hell did I have to think about sex right now? Abstinence for a year...Was it my idea, or Jack's idea or did both of us get tired of being booty partners?*

She grabbed her camisole and then the dark green T-shirt to throw over it. She tucked in the shirt, it was short anyway as she reached for her gun holster. She clipped it to the side of her belt and added the handcuffs and then clipped on her detective shield.

She looked in the mirror and could see the slight bags under her eyes. She hadn't slept well in over a month's time. This killer was making her crazy. She wanted to catch him, well, it. Her friend Margo might be of help to her. After knowing Margo for over three years, she picked up on the woman's odd habits and obsession with wolves. Well, at least she thought it was an obsession. Truth of the matter was that Margo believed in the ability to shift from human to wolf and even other forms. At first she thought her best friend was straight out of a loony bin, but she had to admit that the intensity and knowledge of exactly how people could do this intrigued Dani. Before long, Margo was letting her in on a few secrets going on in society. That information had Dani doing some inquisitive investigating of her own.

That was when she'd noticed the differences in some people she worked with and worked for. There were secret meetings taking place and whispered words or expressions being exchanged, and before long, she found out about certain special groups. She separated gossip from reality and realized that certain detectives, police officers, and even outsiders were chosen by the brass and reassigned to special teams. One of them being the Special Investigations Unit. She was a damn good detective, and being a woman never stopped her from doing her job. A few broken bones, some battle scars, and even a few near-death experiences hadn't driven her away from her dangerous position. But the moment Commander Zespian Fagan introduced himself as the Commander of Special Investigations, she lost her breath and her gut clenched with trepidation. For all she knew, if Margo wasn't a nut job and if what Dani concluded was true, then Zespian had the ability to shift into a wolf and the killer could be one of them.

She swallowed hard and stared at her reflection in the mirror as she brushed back her unruly hair and pulled it into a ponytail. Her muscles flexed. She was built tough and solid. A size ten with hips, ass, and attitude to boot. At five feet seven inches, she was average height, and she felt tough enough to handle most men in most situations. Last night, she wasn't fighting against a man but something different. It was something that made her insides quiver with fear yet there was also some recognition for whatever it was. She needed to speak with Margo.

She grabbed her cell phone off the dresser, unplugging it from the charger in the process. She texted her friend even though it was only 6:30 a.m.

May have a furry situation on my hands. Need info.

A moment later she got a text back.

Shit! Come over now—coffee's hot.

She should have known that Margo was awake. It seemed that woman didn't need much sleep.

Dani grabbed what she needed for work then headed out of her apartment and down four doors to Margo's apartment. She hadn't even knocked on the door when Margo opened it, grabbed Dani's arm, and yanked her inside.

"Hey, what's the rush?" Dani asked as she pulled on her own shirt to readjust it back into position.

Margo looked concerned as her big blue eyes looked Dani over as she sniffed the air around her.

"Okay, Margo, you are freaking me out now. Quit sniffing me. You're acting like a crazy woman."

"You're right. Tell me about the wolf you saw last night." Margo stated as she pulled a chair out by the table and began to take out various canisters filled with different color brown leaves and herbs then set them on the counter in no particular order. At least she hoped they were herbs as Margo began adding different ones to some sort of cooking device with a small flame underneath it.

"That shit better be legal and not drugs, Margo," Dani reprimanded, and Margo didn't even glance up at her with a chuckle or smirk. Something was up.

"Okay, explain what you are doing. I'm the one that saw a wolf last night and you're acting crazy."

Margo looked up as the whistle on the kettle sounded.

"I thought you said the coffee was hot. I hate tea." Dani told her.

"You'll drink the tea, Dani. You'll need all the help you can get."

"Hey, what's that supposed to mean?"

"It means that you're special, Dani. So special in whatever way that this rogue wolf seeks you out. He wants you for himself, Dani. He's going to come for you. I should have seen this coming. "

"What?" Dani exclaimed as she rose from the chair. "You have lost your ever-loving mind, Margo. Enough of the wolf stuff. I shouldn't have texted you. I'm going to be late for work."

"Don't you dare walk out that door. I'll explain it to you, Dani. I'll explain what I know and what I can for now. You're in danger. I smelled him on you immediately."

Dani sniffed her pits. "Smelled who on me?" she asked with her eyebrows crinkled up.

"The wolf from last night. The killer."

"What? But how, he didn't touch me. Wait, I didn't say anything about a killer." Dani stopped short. He hadn't touched her but brushed by her. He hadn't killed her but seemed to toy with her, grazing by her body three times.

"He did touch you, didn't he?" Margo questioned as she poured the hot water over the tea leaves and then slowly wiggled the cup to make the leaves seep into the water.

"Not really. More so grazed my body."

"He was that close to you and didn't take a bite?"

"Hell no. I shot at him, it, whatever it was."

"Wolf. A rogue wolf out of control and possibly out for vengeance. I'm not certain because wolves don't just attack, but soon the others will come. They'll hear of this incident. They probably already know."

"The others? You don't mean other wolves?" Dani panicked as Margo pointed then curled her finger at Dani to come back to the table and drink whatever the hell she mixed in the cup.

"Maybe bad wolves or if you're lucky good ones that can help."

"I don't need help. I'm going to catch this piece of shit and kill it."

Margo wrapped her hand over Dani's arm and squeezed as she held her gaze.

"What I've told you in the past? What I trusted you with and what your investigation on your own has shown you tells you that this is real, Dani. Werewolves exist. There are thousands among us in the city alone. There are some that have more power and influence in that world under those rules that go way beyond any human forms or bureaucracy or law here."

"What in God's name are you talking about?"

"I'll explain. But first, drink the tea. It is a combination of special herbs found elsewhere, out of this country, in fact, that will help to keep your mind sharp and allow your natural abilities to unfold. It's time, Dani. It's time to embrace your heritage and your bloodline."

Dani wasn't certain what Margo was telling her, but as she took a sip of the strange-smelling tea, compelled to believe this insanely wild woman sitting next to her, some odd sensations sparked inside of her. She sipped more, the heat, the stench not bothering her one bit but instead a thirst for more of the hot liquid had her nearly licking the inside of the cup clean. She thought about those feelings she had at the warehouse. She thought about her contact with the dying woman.

"That's it. Perfect. Just as I expected."

"Just as you expected? What?"

"Dani," Margo began to say as she rose from her seat. Margo was a pretty young woman, a few years younger than Dani's twenty-six years, or at least she thought she was young. Sometime Margo spoke with such maturity and wisdom it made Margo seem ancient and it freaked Dani out. By the expression on Margo's face, this conversation was headed into that direction.

"My kind live amongst the humans for many reasons."

"Your kind?"

Margo stared at her, indicating she was getting annoyed with the interruptions, but Dani was getting antsy. She wanted answers, and she wanted to know why she was feeling so odd inside right now.

"Wolves with healing abilities. That's what I am. I am a wolf who comes from a long line of magic. I have the ability to shift and to help heal certain wounds or other ailments that only wolves seem to have."

Dani glanced at the cup and then at Margo who looked incredibly serious.

"Oh shit, Margo. Did you just give me some sort of drug that's going to make me believe the shit your spewing? I have to go to work.

I have a lot of crap to do and a killer to find." Dani began to stand and she felt the dizziness hit her.

"Sit!" Margo yelled. Margo never yelled. She was as quiet as a mouse and a good friend over the years. What the hell was happening here?

"What I say is the truth and you will face the danger head-on soon enough. You are not safe traveling out there on your own. You need my help until your true identity is revealed to you."

"True identity?"

"Yes, Dani. You are not solely human."

"I sure as shit ain't a wolf!" Dani blurted in a panic.

"No, you are not of the wolf, but you do have magic within you. I am not certain of what degree or from which descending line, but if that rogue didn't take a bite out of you or physically touch you, then you could be more powerful than any of us had expected."

"Us?"

"My pack and what is believed to be the pack you were sent to watch over. But it seems you're not the one we were searching for. She's still out there, somewhere. But that is another adventure for another time. Right now I need to find out who you are meant to protect and aid and to what extent your powers extend to."

"You are so freaking me out right now, Margo. Wolves, packs, magic, and family heritages, none of this makes sense to me. I can't be the one you think I am. I have no family, I have no memory of one or of any abilities you believe I have. I've been alone, going from one orphanage to another until Mr. and Mrs. Lynch took me in at age eleven. I don't even have a good relationship with them because I'm such a workaholic. I love my job and I love feeling strong and kicking ass and taking names later. I love it and none of what you're implying makes any sense."

"The Lynches are wonderful people. They are descendants of the Fennigan Pack in Ireland, too. They did a good job protecting you and raising you under their guard. It was a miracle that one of the many other rogues has not sought you out sooner. This has meaning as well. I may need to call in a higher magic official. Perhaps Henry will be available for consultation?"

Margo was talking to herself in front of Dani, making Dani even more concerned.

"The Lynches didn't have any family. That's why they adopted me from St. Mary's orphanage. They were lonely and couldn't have children of their own."

"They were barren. You are right, but they were deeply in love and had total respect and dedication to the Fagan Pack and their generations of warriors and knights. I will try my hardest to give you as much information as possible, but it will be information overload for you. We'll have to get together the next week or so and begin your training. Perhaps that will bring out your true abilities. You have such a strong spirit and brazen personality. I think your battle will be great. Have you noticed anything different lately? I mean, any feelings or inner observations that may show signs of what's to come?"

"I can't take any more of this off-the-wall conversation. I really need to go." Dani stood up. Margo was pulling open a drawer and pulling out a black velvet sachet.

She approached Dani.

"You have no idea how important you are and will be to the were world and to whatever pack you are meant to protect, heal, and possibly guide. You must follow what is inside your heart and your gut. Your instincts, Dani, have saved you and brought you this far in life. There is so much more, Dani. What I tell you is true, and I know you are stubborn, strong-willed, and thickheaded. It makes me crazy with frustration to not know exactly who you are and what your powers will be, but I have done my part. I have watched over you for these three years as those before me have. The time is drawing near. Embrace what is truly yours. Allow the gods to enlighten you. Take this. Wear it at all times until you find your destiny." Margo pulled out a thin chain that contained a crystal star. It was tiny, petite, and the moment Dani put it on, it began to glow purple. Margo covered her mouth and stepped back, bowing to Dani.

"Cut that out. What are you doing and what is this thing?" Dani asked as she touched it. The moment her fingers hit the star the sting of electricity burst up her hand, through her wrist and arm, straight to her heart. She gasped and Margo looked surprised then smiled.

"Amazing."

Dani grabbed the chair and took an unsteady breath. She closed her eyes to stop the dizzy sensations filling her. Instantly, she saw images, numerous ones of both humans and wolves. Again she saw the woman who died before her eyes.

"What is it? What do you see?" Margo asked, whispering next to Dani's ear.

"I see her, the one who died at the warehouse."

"Who was she?"

"A victim of the killer. She was bleeding when I found her. I locked gazes with her and told her that help was on the way. She looked so frightened, but then she heard me and saw my eyes and smiled before she died. I felt as if I helped her somehow, but she died before the paramedics arrived."

"That's it, Dani. That's it, can't you see? You are a healer. You helped her cross over. She was of the wolf and perhaps others there were of the wolf as well."

Dani opened her eyes. She felt her heart beating rapidly, and trepidation tiptoed between her emotions.

"I don't understand. How can that be possible?"

Margo took Dani's hand and squeezed it. Instantly, she felt the fear and confusion disintegrate. Her entire being felt suddenly at peace.

"You must listen to me and embrace your destiny, Dani. It is time."

Dani held Margo's hand as the purple light illuminated again and something deep within Dani changed.

Chapter 3

The brass had insisted Dani take off the next three days, which led to the weekend, so technically she had five days off from work after the incident at the warehouse. She was pissed, and she knew that Margo must have been telling the truth about the secret wolf packs and organizations because she had never seen or heard of the brass that had told her she was off the case for a few days. She also noticed an SUV sitting outside of her apartment complex. Following her gut and this new inner sense she had since swallowing the wild tea Margo gave her, she opted to sneak in the back way and head straight to Margo's place. That was where she hung out for the next three days going over more crazy talk from Margo and more about werewolves, secret orders, princesses, something about circle of elders and Alpha wolves.

They also discussed some possibilities of who the rogue wolf might be and how Dani could kill it.

It was early in the morning on Friday when Dani decided it was time to head back to her apartment. She was going to work whether the brass was happy about it or not. There was a killer out there and about a dozen other cases she was working on with other detectives that needed her attention.

Looking around the hallway, she began to unlock her apartment door then noticed it was already unlocked. Someone may still be in there. She drew her gun and took off the safety.

* * * *

"What the fuck, man. This is not sitting right with me at all. I mean this is a fucking guy's place and my wolf is about to pounce. We should call Van and the others." Miele sat on the couch with a hard-on from hell and his wolf near the surface with need.

"We can't call them. We need to wait until this guy Dani gets here. We'll question him then find out about the woman. If this Detective Dani whatever is fucking our mate, I'm going to rip his fucking heart out," Bently stated.

"Not before I do," Miele replied just as they heard someone by the door to the apartment.

Miele remained in position on the couch. They smelled the place and the detective wasn't a wolf, nor was it their mate, if the scent around the place was any indication. But there was a slight hint of something else. Something he and Bently didn't recognize at all.

* * * *

Dani pushed the door open and raised her gun.

"Who the hell are you?" she blurted out, eyeing the two extremely large men sitting on her couch. The cocky bastards looked quite comfortable.

Their eyes widened in shock and then their nostrils flared as they inhaled wildly.

"Oh shit," one whispered. He was just as big as his buddy. They were wide-shouldered, and indentations in their tight-fitting T-shirts indicated that ripped muscles sat below the fabric. She felt something tingle in her belly.

She was only human, after all, and hadn't had sex in a year. Either way, these two men were very attractive with muscles and tats to boot. She had to give herself a mental kick to remind her that they broke into her apartment.

She gripped her Glock tighter.

"I asked you a fucking question."

"Put the gun down, sweetheart. We're looking for your boyfriend Dani."

Her boyfriend Dani? They thought Dani was a guy. Dumb asses made a stupid assumption. This could play out in my favor.

"Dani's not here. Did he give you a key or do you make it a habit of going around breaking into people's apartments?" she asked as she absorbed their bodies, trying to focus on looking for weapons instead of the bulging cocks they were sporting in those jeans they wore. Damn, the men were big, and why were they turned on by this situation?

Fear gripped her stomach. Were they planning on raping her? Were they wolves that Margo had mentioned might come to take over her case? Her instincts told her that wasn't the case, and it wasn't just because she found them attractive either. She couldn't help but wonder who they were and why she was sexually aroused just from looking at them. Her entire body seemed to hum with acknowledgement. She needed out of this enclosed space and quickly.

"Remain where you are. I'm calling the police. You two assholes can't go around breaking and entering," she began to say, and one guy stood up.

"Don't do that. We're here to see Dani. He knows us."

"Bullshit he knows you."

"Hey, Dani, what's going on? Is everything okay?"

Dani turned toward the doorway where her neighbor Freddy stood with a bag of groceries in his hand.

A glance toward the two big guys and she knew they were pissed.

"You're Dani?" the other guy asked. She grabbed the handle to the door and pulled it closed.

"Get inside your apartment, Freddy." She told her neighbor and she ran down the hallway toward the staircase. She wasn't certain why she ran. She had the gun. She was the cop, but something in her gut warned her, or rather, egged her on to run. What was even fucking crazier was that she hoped they chased her. The thought made her pussy clench and her heart race with anticipation. *What the fuck?*

Just as she descended the third floor, something swooped down from above her. She glanced up in time to see one of the men leap from two floors up and land on his feet in front of her. She was trapped in the corner of the stairwell.

How the hell did he just do that?

She was about to scream, to grab for her weapon when she locked gazes with glowing green eyes.

She was instantly pinned against the wall and now the other big guy stood directly next to the one holding her. Both their eyes glowed and she knew what they were. *Wolves!*

"We're not going to hurt you, Dani. As a matter of fact, we're quite pleased that you're a woman," the one holding her stated.

Her chest heaved up and down. Her nostrils and mouth took in his scent, their scent, and for some odd reason it calmed her and made her vision blur. She closed her eyes as she attempted to calm her breathing.

"Who are you?" she asked in a shaky breath.

"We'll explain, but you need to come with us."

She shook her head.

The one holding her against the wall gave a dirty look.

"I'm Miele and this is my brother Bently. We're with the Special Investigations Unit."

Her eyes widened in shock. They were wolves, and as if they realized that she knew what they were, Miele began to explain.

"Anyone ever tell you not to run from a wolf?"

She shook her head and he leaned his face closer to her. He was damn good looking, which kind of sucked, considering that right now she didn't know if he wanted to rape her, kill her, or just fuck with her head. She tried to tamper down her libido.

"You smell so good, Dani. And I'm so fucking glad that you're not a dude."

He covered her mouth with his. A smoldering, hot kiss that made her forget that the bulging mass of man was a stranger and that he would find her response to his kiss condoning to the action. No, she could not resist, and at the moment didn't care that she was wedged up against the stairwell by a hard muscular body as hands explored her. The panicked feeling began to pull her back to reality, and as he pulled slowly from her lips, his hands on her hips without a care for her revolver or her lack of words, he smiled.

"Fucking delicious."

Her pussy clenched and her face felt hot and flushed from his words. How brazen, animalistic, and hot. His thumbs brushed softly against her torso and he stared down at her. He was fucking toxic. A man as big and attractive as him shouldn't be allowed to roam freely.

Bently now moved into position, taking Miele's place. He gripped her hip and placed his other hand over her neck and under her head to control her body. He winked at her.

"My turn, sweetness." She opened her mouth to reject his move, considering that she just sucked face with his brother, but Bently was already there, kissing the seam of her lips then plunging his tongue deep, exploring her mouth. The kiss was just as hot as his brother's. She was lost in it until Bently trailed the palm of his hand over her hip to her lower back and ass before pressing her hot throbbing pussy against his engorged cock. The reality of the situation jolted her forward, making Bently's lips rip from her own.

She shoved at his chest and moved to the side.

"What in the hell is going on here?" she asked, and both men looked smug.

"Why don't we go back to your apartment? We'll explain." Bently reached for the waist of her pants and rubbed a thumb along her groin. The fucking nerve!

She slapped his hand away.

"I don't think so. I don't want anything to do with you or what you have to say. You had no right kissing me like that, either of you!

This is my case and you're not wanted around here. Leave now, or I will call the police." She stomped up the stairs, surprised when the two men didn't follow, but what was more surprising was the depth of disappointment that filled her belly.

* * * *

As Dani opened the door to the hallway, there stood Margo with her hands on her hips.

"What is going on?" She lowered her voice and leaned forward to whisper, not that anyone else was around them. "I smell wolves everywhere. Alpha wolves."

Then she sniffed again, closer to Dani. Dani felt her cheeks warm as she pressed her hand against Margo's shoulder to make her stop.

"What the hell is an Alpha wolf?"

"OMG! They kissed you. They totally kissed you." She sniffed again and moved around her, smiling wide and practically dancing.

"Two of them right? How was it? Did the earth move? Did your belly go all gaga and other parts, too?"

"Stop it! Nothing happened. I don't want to talk about this. I have to go to work."

The door to the stairs opened and both Miele and Bently entered the hallway. By Margo's gasp of surprise, then the way she lowered her eyes and bowed to the men, Dani had a feeling they were of importance in that were hierarchy Margo had mentioned.

"Give me a break." Dani brushed past Margo and headed toward her apartment. The three followed, but Margo remained behind the men.

That shit was not going to happen to her. Dani Lynch did not bow down to anyone and not any male, wolf, Alpha, or whatever.

Dani walked over to the refrigerator and grabbed a bottle of water.

The two men stared at her with arms crossed in front of massive chests. Margo looked like a mouse ready to be eaten.

"Alphas, may I ask what your business is with Dani?" she whispered with her head still bowed. Dani felt her belly tighten. She knew what their business was with her. They liked her scent and they were wolves that chose women at random to screw around with. Not her. She didn't even date much, she had a booty-call partner to avoid commitments and complications, and Jack was just fine with that, too.

Bently sniffed Margo and then glanced toward Dani. What? Did he want her to act jealous because he was sniffing her best friend?

She gave him an annoyed expression.

"You are from the Fennigan Pack, correct?" Bently asked Margo, and she nodded her head.

He got that from sniffing her? What a crazy wild sense of smell wolves have.

"She is of the magic healing kind. One of the gifted." Miele smiled at her. "Do not be afraid of us. We don't intend any harm to your friend. In fact, we are here to protect her from harm."

"Even more so since it seems she is meant for us," Bently added then winked, and Margo smiled wide.

"She is of importance." Margo began to say.

"Margo! That's enough." Dani interrupted then walked toward her friend. She grabbed her arm.

"Will you two excuse us, please? You can leave or you can make yourselves at home, since you did that earlier without an invite." Margo gasped and the two wolves chuckled as they stood watching her drag Margo into the other room.

"Can they hear me if I whisper?" she asked Margo.

"Not all the way in here. What is your problem? You just hit the jackpot in hot men for life. Those two are part of the Fagan Pack. They're big shots and there are five of them. Holy shit, Dani, you are going to be their healer and perhaps protector or something just as grand as soon as we figure it out. We have to explain what's going on."

"No!" Dani interrupted. "You are not going to tell them anything. I am not destined for anything with them. I am destined to be independent, single, and working on catching killers, one in particular at the moment."

"Dani, you can't deny your destiny."

"I am in charge of my destiny. I will make the decisions in my life and not be forced to bow my head and walk behind a bunch of men who can change into wolves. That is not for me."

Margo looked insulted, Dani realized, and she tried to back step.

She placed her hand on her shoulder. "I'm sorry, Margo. I know this all means so much to you, but I'm human and I have worked hard for my independence and for the life I lead. I am not a submissive person."

Margo smiled. "You do not understand but soon you will. I will respect your wishes, Dani, because we are great friends and I love you. But know that those men are meant to be yours and not to control you or make demands upon you but to protect and love you."

"Whatever. I don't have time for this mumbo jumbo stuff. I'm wasting time. I'm going down the fire escape. Keep them busy for me."

Dani opened the window and looked down. It was only four floors high. The fire escape was sturdy enough, so she made her descent down the metal steps.

Margo would ensure she got the time needed to get to her car.

* * * *

Margo reentered the living room to find both Alphas pacing.

"Where is she?" Miele Fagan asked abruptly. She winced at his tone. His brother Bently walked closer.

"Margo, you know why we are here. She is important to us. She is our mate."

Margo covered her mouth and her eyes widened. This wasn't good. Dani was going to flip out. Shit! They were going to flip out when they realize she ran.

"Um, that is amazing," she began to say when Miele jumped up and grabbed her arm.

"Where is she?" he demanded to know. She knew Alphas and the Fagan Pack had seriously intense reputations. They had killed many wolves before to protect the circle of elders.

She bowed her head.

"I am sorry, Alpha, but she is gone."

"What?" Bently ran toward the bedroom and returned a moment later.

"She went down the fire escape."

"The fire escape? She could have broken her freaking neck," Miele reprimanded, and Bently shook his head.

"If she returns before we find her, you call us and you do not warn her first, Margo, or there will be consequences. One phone call, or your Alpha will step in."

Margo gasped at Miele's threat.

"Yes, Alphas." She bowed her head and they hurried out the door.

* * * *

Dani jumped into her Mustang, started it up, and took off down the main street. She caught the red light at the intersection and kept looking in the rearview mirror to see if they were pursuing her. No sign of them yet. She released an uneasy breath and swallowed the lump of guilt she felt.

Why should I feel guilty? I didn't do anything wrong. They kissed me. They wanted to have sex with me because they're wolves! Fuck if any of this makes sense.

She jumped as she heard her cell phone ringing.

Answering it, she heard Jack's voice and another string of guilt hit her belly. But why. It wasn't like they were dating or boyfriend and girlfriend. They hadn't even had sex in nearly a year. The thought that he wasn't her booty call anymore made her feel crappy. They'd drifted apart, too. She just wasn't good at relationships.

"What's up, stranger?" she asked, trying to pretend normalcy and ignore the negative feeling she had. She stepped on the gas and caught the next light a block up from her place.

"Nothing, sweetheart. Just, I heard about you getting taken off the case."

"I'm not off the case. The brass made me take a few days off to clear my head. I was covered in human blood. It was shitty."

"I know. I fucking heard. I did call you. You should answer those voice mails."

"I know. I did but didn't get a chance to respond. I appreciate the call, though."

"Well, I just heard that some guys from a Special Investigations Unit are being assigned to the case."

"What? Were their names Miele and Bently?"

"No, some other guys. Big fucking dudes, too, Dani. I mean, like, over six feet, big muscles, tattoos, and total military types."

"Shoot. I guess our paths will cross eventually."

"Yeah, I'm sure they will. You won't miss them. All the chicks around the department were practically drooling. Something about the guys' good looks and shit."

She swallowed hard.

"Got a last name?"

"Yeah it was Fagan or Fagarn and they're brothers or cousins. Some crazy shit. Anyway, watch your ass. I hear this killer is really bad. He must be for the brass to be calling in reinforcements like military personnel."

"I appreciate the heads-up. I'll be by in a few hours. I'm checking out my own leads," she told him.

"I can come over tonight if you don't have plans?"

"I'll think about it."

"Hey, I didn't mean to not call you. I kind of met someone and then things didn't work out. I wouldn't do that to you. You know, call you for one reason while I'm interested in someone else, even though we had an agreement."

"No sweat, Jack. It's cool and you don't owe me any explanations. It's been, like, a year."

"I know it's crazy. I'm sorry to assume that you would be interested. A hot babe like you has to be seeing someone."

She chuckled.

"I'll call you if I'm free." She disconnected the call and felt a little better about clearing the air between her and Jack, but she also felt shitty. She just wasn't good with opening up her heart and connecting with a man on an intimate level. It was complicated and involved too much energy and giving too much of herself. She liked being alone. Well, at least most of the time, and she didn't want to just have sex to have sex anymore. But damn did the two wolves back there know how to kiss a woman. She felt it to her fucking toes. That was wild because right now she should be freaking out knowing that there were wolves living among humans. She swallowed hard. In her mind, she knew that she believed it back then. Back when Margo had told her they existed. Dani kept a watchful eye out at the precinct. She could tell that private meetings were taking place, and also she believed there were even private meeting rooms. This was like some off-the-wall spy movie meets sci-fi craziness.

She shook her head and continued down the road. As she glanced at her reflection in the mirror, she noticed a blush to her cheeks. The reality was, wolf or not, she was definitely attracted to Miele and Bently. She'd have to be dead not to be and her pussy sure the hell wasn't dead. In fact, her panties were wet from thinking about them. She tried to adjust her ass in the seat and her holster rubbed along the side of the seat belt.

The sound of her cell phone chiming took her mind off of the hotties and back to reality.

She pressed the button on the hands-free device so she could answer the call.

"Hello, I'm looking for Detective Lynch."

"This is Detective Lynch. Who is this please?"

"My name is Baily May. I've been watching the television about the murders taking place around the city. My cousin April was one of the women killed last month."

"I'm so sorry to hear that. How can I help you, Baily?" It wasn't uncommon for members of a victim's family to call the detectives in charge of their cases. It sometimes helped the victims bring closure of some degree to their family member's death.

"Well, I don't know if it's anything to be concerned about, but the detectives at your precinct said you wouldn't mind if I called you."

"Go on, Baily, it's okay. Tell me what's bothering you."

"I was sitting at the coffee shop. I hadn't gone since before April was killed, but we used to go there together often. She mentioned a club on Chester Street that she had gone to a few times. Anyway, while I was sitting there, I saw some weird-looking guy talking to two young women. One of the women got up and walked outside with him. They talked a bit and anyway, he handed her a card. I think I saw him at the coffee shop before. In fact, a few days before my sister disappeared, the man was talking with her by the table but then I arrived. Well, today when I saw him, I didn't know what to do or whether or not to approach him, and then he happened to turn and look right at me. It was so strange. I swear you're probably going to think I'm crazy, Detective Lynch, but I think I saw his eyes glowing."

Dani nearly crashed her car. She pulled over to the side of the road and asked Baily to repeat the last part. She then took down a description of the man and the time of day Baily saw him when she was with her sister and then she wrote down today's time. It was a good hour difference.

"Do you think it could be the killer?" Baily asked.

"I'm not sure, Baily, but believe me, I'll do my best to figure this out. I may need you to sit down and do a composite sketch. I'll need something to go by when I stake out that coffee shop."

"Okay. I'll cooperate. I want April's killer to be caught. I don't want to hear another story about another innocent person murdered."

"I understand. Can you meet me at the department or would you like me to have an artist meet you somewhere else?"

"I'm a little scared now. I don't want him to find me."

"Give me your address. I'll personally come along with the sketch artist, okay?"

"Thank you."

"I'll see you soon."

Dani got off the phone and took an unsteady breath. Could this be the lead she'd been waiting for? She also needed to check out that club on Chester. She knew the one. It was a big place. If her memory served her correctly, there had been a few strange incidents over the years there, and usually one of the special task forces was called in. She punched in the number to someone in the department that did sketch work. He would meet her at Baily's.

Chapter 4

"You let her, a human, get the slip on you?" Van asked as they all stood around the meeting room at the department. No one had seen Dani anywhere and Miele and Bently just arrived.

They looked upset and Van had the feeling that something was up. As soon as the brass left the room, Van demanded answers.

"What the fuck really happened?" Van asked.

"She's our fucking mate," Miele stated and they all stood up from their lounging positions.

"Say that again." Baher took a step toward Miele and Bently.

"You heard him. We were shocked, too. First that Dani was a she, not a he, and second that she's our mate," Bently stated.

"What is she like?" Baher asked.

"Here's a picture of her," Van stated as he clicked a button on the laptop and Dani's face came up on the full-screen board in the front of the room.

A long, slow whistle went through the room.

"Fucking beautiful," Baher whispered.

Van knew she was beautiful and highly intelligent. The current picture showed her wearing tapered black dress pants that hugged her shapely figure. The holster and gun, badge, and other paraphernalia sat against her waist. She had long brown hair that was pulled back and into a braid down her back. From the picture, she appeared to have light-green eyes.

"It states that she's twenty-six years old and has been a detective for five years now with more than sixty closed cases under her belt. That's impressive," Van stated.

"She's top notch. Received numerous awards in the police academy, graduating top in her class. She has a high success rate of closed cases in her file, and hey, Randolph, she's got a thing for guns," Van teased their quiet, very serious brother.

"Interesting," Randolph stated. His eyes never left the screen.

"She smells incredible, too, and her lips, damn," Bently added.

"Her lips? You fucking kissed her?" Van asked.

"We both did. Couldn't resist doing it. Nor would you if you were there," Miele added.

"No wonder she fucking ran. You two playboys probably scared her." Baher ran his hand through his hair.

"She knows that wolves exist," Bently told them, and they all looked right at him.

"What? How can she?" Van asked, now really concerned for their well-being.

"She's best friends with a magic healer," Miele informed his brothers.

"Yeah, from the Fennigan Pack," Bently added.

"The Fennigan Pack? What the heck is she doing living in New York? The Fennigan Pack's been busy in Ireland helping to restore the Order along with Ava and the Declan brothers," Van replied.

"There's a reason for everything, Van. We all realize that. My main concern is this rogue wolf. I'm not certain that he's working alone. I'm not even sure why he's killing these people," Miele stated.

"We haven't come up with any connections between the victims. Over at the crime scene, in the warehouse, we came up with shit," Van explained.

"The one thing we know for sure is that this wolf or whatever kills violently. It has no control over its anger. It is wild, nearly causing complete destruction to the human body. That in itself has raised so many red flags in the departments that we have to take over the investigation," Baher stated.

"The pictures from the crime scene were that bad, Van?" Bently asked, and Van nodded his head.

"We had to call in a few wolves to get rid of more than half the bodies and replace them with human ones from the morgue. Otherwise, the coroner's office could have realized something was different about the bodies, their blood type, organs, et cetera. It was a fucking close call. We also got lucky and Sarah from Tolga pack was the coroner on duty. She got rid of the human and covered for us."

"We need to find Dani. If she were to stumble upon this killer…" Miele began to say then turned toward Bently.

"We do this together. Baher, make the call. Get her cell phone number and accounts open. See if she made any calls since leaving the apartment. Bently, you call in to our men and have them locate her vehicle. We'll track her down and take her to our place and explain to her that she can't run from us and she can't continue with the investigation," Van ordered and everyone moved about the room, pulling out cell phones and making calls.

Van looked at Randolph.

"What, Randolph?"

"She may know about wolves, but she doesn't know what she's dealing with. This thing is not like us."

Randolph looked away from Van and out toward the window and the city skyline.

His brother was a man of few words. He was always deep in thought or silent. He had been like that for so many years, never showing emotion or an effect from even the heaviest of violence around him. Van had the same fears that Randolph did. They were together when they saw the massive amount of blood, the pictures of the torn flesh and violence. They were worried that this killer could blow their covers and make the humans aware of the existence of their kind. It needed to be stopped, and they would be the ones to stop it.

Chapter 5

He knew that he should have killed the brunette. In his sane mind, he was aware that what he was doing needed to be controlled better, but he was losing that control too quickly now. He glanced around him, being sure to avoid the cameras by the front entrance to the apartment building. He needed to find more of that special blood, that scent that was all consuming. Detective Dani Lynch had it. The moment her fear wafted through the air in the warehouse, he knew that she was special. The smoke, the blood from the other worthless bodies couldn't hide her scent. He needed to find her. Dani would first serve him and then his master. Although everything about her yelled "human," there was something inside him that wanted her, needed her in every respect. It was strong enough to grab his full attention, and even now, just thinking about her made his hunger grow stronger.

He entered the apartment building, knowing that Baily's blood could hold him over a bit longer. It wasn't like he was a vampire that needed to feast on blood to survive. It was a side effect of the transformation Dr. Evans had conducted. The doctor should have known better than to try to trick a vamp into giving him blood. The vamp he chose probably tainted it with something. Perhaps just the incredible urge to get blood, drink it, and kill for it.

He didn't want to think about it. The need was far beyond his control unless the doctor's idea was correct. A healer, with powers strong enough to fight even vampires existed, and he prayed that Dani was the one with such powers. He had no idea what that scent was until he felt that urge to kill and take more blood eased in her presence. He was almost hypnotized by her powers, but it seemed she hadn't a clue what she was doing. That was perfect. She was pure, untouched, and he would use that once she was in his possession and under his control.

He had a new hunger growing. It ran deep through his bloodstream and straight to his soul. He practically felt his incisors expand. Dani was the one he had searched so long for. If he told his master, then he would want her for himself. No way was that going to happen. Dani's scent was all consuming, enticing to the point that he wanted to fuck her, plant his seed in her special womb, and keep her as his own forever. He couldn't let the master know about her. Not yet. Perhaps not ever, because he knew how evil his master was. Dr. Evans would want to experiment on Dani and use her for his own personal achievements and advances. The wolf growled low. She belonged to him and not the master and not anyone else. She could cure him of his need for blood. His kind needed special care. He would prove to his master that he wasn't an experiment gone badly, but a gift so powerful that he would lead the way. No one would ever try to control him again.

* * * *

Dani and the sketch artist, Martin, knocked on the apartment door. Baily wasn't answering, and Dani was feeling concerned.

"Should we call it in, Detective?" Martin asked.

"With what has been going on with the murders, yeah, I don't want to take a chance," she whispered as Martin took a few steps away from the door. He called the department, whispering their location and situation when suddenly the door he was next to opened, and Martin was pulled inside at record speed.

Dani's gun was drawn and she yelled, "Police!"

A body came flying back out as she began to approach the doorway. It happened so damn fast she thought it couldn't be real, but it was real. The body hit the other wall and fell to the rug. There was blood everywhere. Martin's throat was slashed open.

She abruptly turned around as a huge growl echoed from the room. The wolf, the monster she'd caught a glimpse of from the warehouse, was there. He showed his face, lifted his claws prepared to strike, and she fired, one, two shots and nothing happened. All that did was enrage him. She turned to run, knowing that if bullets from her Glock wouldn't kill him, then she didn't have a chance.

Dani slammed the door opened and it was on her fast. It slashed at her side, causing her to scream then lower for cover from another strike. The pain radiated down her arms. It burned so badly, and the force sent her into the wall. She grabbed onto the railing and then another strike to the back of her head sent her tumbling down the stairs. She screamed and yelled with every step she slammed over.

"Dani!" She heard someone yelling her name as she turned toward the landing then back up toward the monster. It vanished.

The next thing she saw was blood covering the steps she had just stumbled down and then movement to her right. She had no way of defending herself now, with her arms underneath her and her face planted against the concrete floor.

"Dani! Fuck, are you okay?"

She looked up and saw Bently, and Miele was right behind him.

Relief flooded her body as she closed her eyes and took an unsteady breath.

"Don't move, baby. Just lie still," Bently whispered.

"Is it up there, Dani? Is the wolf still there?" Miele asked as he began to make his way up the staircase. She shook her head.

"He's gone. He killed Martin."

Dani tried to move despite Bently's command. His tone, the way his large hands, so masculine and thick caressed so gently, soothed her. It was strange and it felt as if it eased the sharp, burning pain against her ribs and under her breast.

"You're bleeding. What from?" Bently asked, trying to gently move her, but Dani resisted his help. She was fine. She would get up on her own and she would tend to her wound on her own. If only the dizziness would pass. Her head was throbbing and she felt so sick to her stomach.

"I think she hit her head," one of them stated, and then the other cursed.

"What are you so mad about? I'm the one in pain," she whispered.

"Let me see?" Bently stated then began to gently check her head for the injury.

"Cool it. I can handle it." As she began to lift herself up into a sitting position, the pain increased, and the door to the staircase swung open hard. From above, more noise and action began. But she was swiftly losing her sense of awareness.

Don't pass out. Fucking don't pass out.

"Hey, you got her?" Another man yelled from the top of the staircase. She locked gazes with him. Holy shit was he big. As his eyes locked with hers, she felt a jolt of awareness. He looked so much like Bently, it was wild.

His eyebrows crinkled as he sniffed the air. "This her blood?" he asked, almost sounding annoyed that she'd messed up the stairs with her blood. She also didn't like how these men were talking as if she couldn't speak for herself. Then she realized she must be in some kind of shock because she really hadn't explained anything or said much at all. Was she stating things out loud?

Oh God, I hope I didn't say out loud how fucking hot they are.

That damn beast nearly killed me and slammed my head so hard I can't even defend myself right now. Shit!

She glanced down at her side and could see the blood penetrating her badly torn shirt.

"Son of a bitch!" she stated then got to her knees. She took a series of deep breaths.

"Hold her still. She's hurt," the one at the top of the stairs stated.

"Are the others on their way? Is it secure yet, Randolph?" Bently asked as both he and Miele began to help Dani get up. Now she knew the other guy's name. My God they were impressive-looking men, superior in every aspect. How would they look as wolves? The thought made her think of the beast that assaulted her and killed two innocent people upstairs. They could lose it just as easily.

She pushed their hands away and scooted back toward the wall, using it to push up against so she could stand up.

"What's going on in here? We've got team three moving in and team five surrounding the area. The third floor is secure."

Another one? How many of them were there in this little group?

"She's injured, Baher. We need to get her medical attention," Bently stated.

"Bently, you and Miele take her through the exit in the back. Van is giving out the orders upstairs. We need to get her to safety."

Her vision began to blur and she fell back down to the floor, her legs out in front of her.

"I'm not going anywhere with any of you." Her last words sounded like a whisper, and then she lost focus completely and passed out.

Chapter 6

The sound of mumbled voices awoke her from her sleep. Dani blinked her eyes open, the movement causing pain in her head. Her lids felt so damn heavy, all she wanted to do was sleep. She tried to force herself to wake up and to clearly see the people who were talking. She closed her eyes as their voices became clearer.

"It was a close call in all respects. She could have been killed. The humans could have arrived on scene in the midst of that mess."

"Well, thanks to us tracking her cell phone and then the 9-1-1 call that came through, we got there fast enough. But that piece of shit got away with killing again. I just can't figure out what he's after."

Dani tried to figure out who was talking. She recognized Bently's voice but not the other one. The second voice was firm, authoritative and kind of sharp. He sounded in charge.

She tried to adjust her body then moaned as the sharp pain hit her ribs. Her eyes blinked open.

"You're okay, Daniella. You're in a safe place with men that can protect you." She heard the voice and looked at the man standing beside her bed, dressed in a white shirt. He smiled, and when he reached for her to touch her cheek, she tightened up in fear of his touch, and the pain hit again.

"I'm not going to hurt you," he whispered.

"Who are you?" she asked then coughed. Her throat felt really dry, and she attempted to sit up.

"Whoa, baby, don't move around so much, you'll reinjure yourself," said another man who now leaned across the bed on the opposite side.

She blinked her eyes a few more times, clearing her vision.

She clutched the sheet to her body. She was naked underneath. Her shock and anger were apparent as one of the men spoke up.

"Don't freak out. The doctor had to view your injuries. He's our cousin, so it's okay."

"Um, how the hell does that make it okay?" she demanded as she absorbed the two men on either side of her and now a third that entered through the doorway.

"We'll explain once you're feeling better."

She looked at them. The one to her right, who was doing all the talking, had stunning hazel eyes. They were just as stunning as Miele's, as she recalled.

"You'll explain now, starting with who the hell you are," she stated firmly, and they appeared surprised. *Well, la-di-da, welcome to the real world where women actually have rights and don't bow down to wolves or sexy hot soldiers.*

"I'm Baher, Miele and Bently's brother. This is Charlie, my cousin, the doctor who cared for your wounds, and over there by the doorway, the big guy, is Randolph."

She glanced toward the one called Randolph. He looked downright mean. His arms were crossed in front of his chest, his eyes appeared black and threatening, and she didn't like the jolt of awareness she felt straight to her pussy. His olive shirt stretched way across his wide chest. Damn, was he big. Did wolves take steroids?

Holy shit, I'm losing my fucking mind.

"I think Charlie can leave," Randolph stated as he stared at his cousin. Instead of looking taken aback, Charlie smiled.

"You're going to be fine. Your men will take care of you and they know how to get in touch with me," Charlie told her. Her mind was fuzzy. More fuzzy and unclear than she felt. Did he say "your men?"

He left the room and Randolph only moved a second to let his cousin pass. He looked pretty pissed off at his cousin, and once Charlie left, Randolph walked into the room. Her belly tightened and she clutched the sheets against her then glanced around the room. *How the hell am I going to make a run for it?*

She saw her boots, her jeans, and her guns lying on the chair. For men who were holding her captive, they were stupid to leave her weapons lying out like that. She always carried two guns. One on her hip and one on her ankle as backup.

"Don't even think about it, Daniella. We are not here to hurt you. As soon as you're fully awake, we'll explain," Baher stated, and she turned toward him and those gorgeous hazel eyes.

They stood out so much against his tan complexion.

She tried to sit up and Baher and Randolph reached for her. She cringed from the pain and from the sticky tape holding the large bandage against her ribs.

"What the hell?"

Randolph scooped her up as Baher fixed the pillow.

"Hey, I can—"

One look from Mr. Intense Randolph and she closed her mouth. She didn't even freak when the sheet that covered her breasts moved lower, exposing half of her areola. She prayed that neither man noticed her hard nipples, her body a sure giveaway to her attraction to them. Instead, Randolph softly pulled the sheets up. She was surprised at the gentleness for such a large brute of a man, covered in tattoos, and then he caressed his thumb over her nipple through the sheet.

Her lips parted and her pussy clenched.

They locked gazes, and the intensity of his stare was intimidating, big-time. She took a slow, uneasy breath.

"Beautiful." He told her with no change of facial expression.

Randolph walked out of the room, and Dani shook her head.

"He's a man of few words, Dani. But the words he chooses to say are most important and true." Baher took position by the side of the bed.

"Are you more comfortable now?" Baher asked.

She looked at him and nodded. Randolph had knocked her speechless.

This guy Baher sat down on the side of the bed, his thigh lightly touching hers through the sheet. He had wide shoulders and defined muscles. He also was sporting some tattoos just like Randolph. She could immediately see the resemblance to his brothers Bently and Miele. The brown color of their hair was nearly identical and their eye color similar. It was easy to tell that they were siblings, even their height was the same, except for Randolph. He was a bit extra large and about two inches taller than Baher and Bently's six feet three inches.

He placed his hand over her waist and onto the sheets right next to her hip. A blanket of warmth penetrated through her body.

She tightened up and held his gaze. The physical attraction she felt mirrored the same she had for Randolph, Bently, and Miele.

"You're going to be fine. It was a close call back there." He reached up to touch a finger under her chin as he smiled.

His thumb brushed gently along her bottom lip.

"You're going to have some bruising from the fall. My God, you could have broken your neck from tumbling down that staircase." The intensity in his voice increased, and his finger stilled against her chin. He was mere inches from her.

"I didn't want to get eaten," she snapped at him, and he chuckled then scooted forward.

He stared at her and it made her feel aroused. She didn't even know this guy, just that he was brothers with Miele and Bently. The two men had kissed her, and now their brother looked like he was about to kiss her, too.

"Randolph was right, Daniella, you are quite beautiful."

She absorbed the firmness of his lips, his superior jaw structure and handsome features right before his lips touched down upon her own. His kiss was soft, sweet, a total tease to her sexual appetite that seemed to grow more and more as she met the Fagan men. How many did Margo say there were?

Margo?

Baher released her lips and smiled softly. "Thank you."

"Thank me for what?"

"For allowing me to kiss you."

She shyly turned away from him. "I need to get up. I have to make some phone calls. I need to check on my friend Margo and the department."

"No phone calls." She looked up as a firm, abrupt voice growled through the room. *Holy shit, who is that?*

She swallowed hard and grabbed hold of the sheet, clinging to it like a security blanket. She wished she could reach her guns or something for support. She felt vulnerable, especially since she was naked beneath the sheets.

"Baher, they need you downstairs."

"No problem, Van." Dani reached for Baher's arm as he began to get up. He must have sensed her unease at leaving her with the Van guy.

"It's okay, baby. That is Van, our Alpha and oldest brother. He will ensure your protection as well." Baher leaned in and kissed her cheek then rose from the bed. As he was walking out, she noticed him whisper something to Van, and something in Van's eyes changed a moment then disappeared. It was very quick but she noticed it.

The man was just as large as Randolph, but he had black hair and oh-so-very-gorgeous green eyes. He moved toward her and looked her over. *Holy shit, his eyes had power of some sort because she felt a warm, almost burning sensation against her body, following the path of his eyes*

"You feel okay to sit up? You have bruises everywhere on your body."

She swallowed hard. How come they all knew that?

"What, was I on display for you and your brothers as your cousin treated my injuries?" she asked, now feeling embarrassed and annoyed, not because she thought they were perverts but because she was self-conscious about her body. She was five feet seven inches tall, kind of big-boned and muscular from working out. She didn't have defined, tight abs or anything, and she was far from dainty. Although, compared to these men, she was a dwarf.

He crossed his arms in front of his chest and stared down at her.

"There are things we need to explain to you. We'll discuss what we know and think you should be privy to and take the proper precautions necessary."

"Excuse me, but what do you mean by privy to? If you're talking about this case, my case, then you you'd better think again, buddy."

He gave her the evil eye with those dark green eyes of his. Son of a bitch did that turn her on.

"You do not realize the seriousness of this situation, Daniella."

"It's Dani," she stated firmly. So far, Bently and Miele called her Dani, but the others, Randolph, Baher, and Van felt it necessary to use her full name. She hated to admit that it turned her on, the way they said her name and especially with such authority and power. This was bad. It was very, very bad. Already, she felt her defenses lowering. It had something to do with the macho testosterone in the men. Their good looks, authoritative attitudes, and superb bodies were irresistible. She needed to focus and remain somewhat in charge, despite their tactics.

How did they know my full name anyway? Son of a bitch, they looked in my file. They investigated me.

She took a deep breath about to rip into king shit over there when he stopped her.

His hand, palm forward, came up and then he began.

"First and most importantly, you are our mate. My brothers and I will do everything in our power to protect you. Life as you know it will change and we'll be moving back to Texas once we clear up this wolf situation. Secondly, for some wild reason, this rogue, deranged wolf wants to kill you or keep you. He wants you for some reason, and it seems to be beyond just to take your blood or rip your heart out. That concerns me greatly. There is also a special scent about you. It is something that calls especially to each of our wolves but may be the reason this creature seeks you out. That places you in danger and we can't allow that."

Was he fucking serious? Move to Texas? Mates? Scent of some sort? *Holy shit, I've entered the Twilight Zone!*

"Excuse me, chief, but what if I'm not interested in your protection, or in believing any of this bullshit you're spewing? I don't appreciate you telling me that I smell and that some murderous, hideous-looking monster wants me because of it."

"I did not say that you smell, Daniella."

"Dani!" she yelled.

He raised his eyebrows at her and she closed her lips.

"I will explain further once you're feeling better."

"Oh, I feel great. As a matter of fact, I feel like getting up and getting out of here."

Dani cringed as she tossed back the sheets in anger and stood up. She completely forgot about being naked and about having injuries and bruises. This man got under her skin in a flash. She couldn't think straight.

His arms were around her in an instant, assisting her.

"Damn it, Daniella, you cannot be jumping out of bed with your injuries."

She held his waist, the rough texture of his jeans brushed erotically against her aroused body pats. Damn, she was so fucking horny and had no idea why. Did they give her something?

She was breathing heavy and it seemed to have more to do with her sudden sexual desires than her injuries. She gripped his waist and slowly looked up toward him.

He stared at her straight-faced. "What you're feeling is normal. Soon enough we will each ease that ache."

"Excuse me? I don't know what you're talking about. You lost me and I want to leave."

"You're not leaving."

"Did you drug me?" she asked, and he shook his head as if annoyed with her childish question.

"Of course not. You passed out from the trauma of the attack and your injuries. Charlie gave you something to numb the area where he stitched you up."

"Stitches? I have stitches?" she asked, stepping back, off-balance again as she tried to look down at the bandages.

Van held her firmly by her hips. She felt her breasts bounce and the reality of her nakedness quickly sank in.

She swallowed hard and hoped that her cheeks weren't as red as they felt. With what dignity she had left, she straightened her shoulders and lifted her chin.

"I would like some clothing, please." She swallowed hard. She saw his eyes were glowing and he kept his mouth closed tight. Taking a small step back, he pulled off his black T-shirt and then placed it on her.

Was he fucking serious?

The scent of him filled her body, her nostrils, and her entire being. It was outrageous, but she felt wrapped in him. She closed her eyes, and then she felt his hands on her hips.

Looking up toward him, her eyes barely opened all the way as a feeling of drunkenness nearly overtook her as he spoke.

"You are our mate, Daniella. Do not fight the sensations you are feeling."

She could hardly make out his massive chest filled with muscles. The intricate tattoos expanded over his breast, shoulder, and down his arm over muscle upon muscle. She imagined licking across his skin, tasting every inch of him, all of him, unmarked or inked up.

He leaned down and cupped her neck and head then slowly, confidently moved closer. She anticipated the feel of his lips and wondered if they would be soft or rough. When he kissed her lips, she knew she sensed his dominance and masculinity. She was in a real man's arms. She felt his other hand caress along her backside, molding her front to his front. Her very wet pussy pressed against his jean-covered cock, and she wanted him. Oh God, did she want him.

His kiss grew deeper as he made love to her mouth and held her body against his own. The fabric of his T-shirt teased her nipples to the point of causing her to moan. He released her lips slowly, trailing kisses down her neck to her shoulder. One hand remained holding her ass snug against his cock while he used the other to cup her breast. He had incredibly large hands.

"Oh God, what is wrong with me?"

"Absolutely nothing." He pinched her nipple as he nibbled on her neck with his teeth. When he slowly pulled back, indicating he was done tasting her, she opened her eyes and locked gazes with him. His green eyes were glowing like that of a wolf and his incisors looked elongated. It was wild and crazy as she gasped and tried to retreat. His hold was firm, and when he spoke, his voice was slightly distorted.

"Don't be afraid. It is you that brings my wolf to surface, tests my ability to maintain control, when all I want to do is sink my cock deep into your pussy and become part of you."

Holy fuck, what am I supposed to say to that?

She swallowed hard.

"I don't know what to say. I never…"

He pulled back and steadied her by her hip bones.

"There's plenty of time to explain. Would you like to shower? I can help you."

She sniffed the air then scrunched her eyebrows. "Do I really smell that badly?" He was giving her a complex.

He chuckled then pulled her against his chest.

"Not bad, but that good."

He picked her up gently in his arms and carried her toward the bathroom.

* * * *

By the grace of God, Dani took a shower and actually felt slightly better. She used the soap and lathered it nice and thick so maybe these men wouldn't keep referring to her as having a scent of some kind easily detected. She went over the day's events in her head combined with bits of information Margo had shared about wolves in general. Alphas were superior. She got that, totally could see that with all five of the men and especially Van and Randolph. She thought about the sketch artist from the department, about Baily and the fact that the killer knew where she was headed. How the hell did it know that? Was it really after her now? Could this have something to do with what Margo told her? Did Dani actually possess some kind of healing power for wolves? Well, not any wolves, but the Fagan Pack wolves. Well, maybe others as well. She thought about the woman who died in the warehouse. She swallowed, feeling the thickness in her throat as her belly growled with hunger. This was too much to take in. The men were overwhelming her on top of all the rest of the stuff. Her head ached and she closed her eyes a moment, letting the hot water run over her body.

She rinsed, being careful to avoid getting the bandage wet best she could. That fucking beast nearly ripped her breast off. It gave her the chills. Her bullets hadn't done shit to it. There had to be a way to kill it. She needed to be armed and ready to defend herself. Her gun brought her feelings of safety and power. Without it, she felt naked and lost. She wasn't giving that monster another chance. Next time she would kill that beast. Perhaps the men would know how.

She saw that the bandages were not holding up well, despite the plastic coating. She probably shouldn't have showered yet, but the way they referred to her scent being so strong and different didn't sit right with her. Charlie had covered the stitches with some kind of plastic to keep it dry. As she dried off, she noticed that the edges were coming off. She probably shouldn't have showered that long, but she scrubbed her body thoroughly with concern over the scent she was apparently omitting. But with the soap being unscented, which made no sense to her at all, she had scrubbed her skin triple time. She didn't want the stitches to get infected. She panicked and then she heard the knock on the door.

She held the towel against her body as the door opened slowly.

"Daniella, are you okay?" Van asked in a very deep voice that seemed to travel over her oversensitive body.

Get a grip, woman. You don't need this kind of trouble.

"I'm just drying off. Um...are there any more bandages around?"

The door opened further and Van entered, his expression filled with concern. Just as she began to ask what he thought he was doing, Baher joined him.

Both men were dressed in black camo pants and were wearing black T-shirts stretched across their muscles. She swallowed hard as they ate up the space between them and her.

She clutched the towel tighter and took a retreating step back, nearly falling into the tub.

"Stop! Both of you, right there!" Both men froze. She held the towel with one hand, and all it seemed to be covering was her pussy.

"Damn, Dani, let us help you with that. The bandages are coming undone," Baher stated as he walked around her and over toward a closet in the far corner. She turned a little sideways, giving Van a clear view of her right ass cheek and thigh as she watched to see what Baher was up to.

He ran his hand through that brown hair of his then stretched up, causing his biceps to peek out further from the confinement of his shirtsleeve. Her eyes roamed over every delicious inch of him as he stretched farther. The move exposed more tattoos, and she licked her lips.

My God, the man has a great ass.

She heard Van clear his throat, and when she looked back at him, his arms were crossed in front of his chest and his one eyebrow rose up. He caught her staring at his brother. Well, drooling was more like it.

Baher returned with a large first aid kit in hand.

"Okay. Leave it on the counter and get out," she told them, and they ignored her. They actually ignored her. Baher placed the box on the counter then knelt down in front of her, placing his hand on her thigh and the towel. His hazel eyes stared up at her.

"Let me see it," he told her in a very calm voice that sent goose bumps over her flesh. He was even better looking close up, and he smelled great, too.

She shook her head. *Now I'm fucking smelling them like they've smelled me.*

"Listen to him now," Van stated firmly with his arms still crossed in front of him and a scowl mean as could be on his face. She swallowed hard and lifted her chin.

"No. I'm a big girl, and I can take care of myself."

"Those days are over. We're taking care of you now," Van snapped at her.

She was shocked, outraged, and nearly speechless, and, double damn it, turned on by his tone and words. She needed to fight this. She was an independent woman.

"I don't think so, Van."

Baher placed the palm of his large hand against her thigh and she gasped. She couldn't stop him with one hand while her other hand held the towel in place.

Baher gently pressed his hand against her skin then slowly moved upward under the towel. Her belly muscles tightened, her legs felt as if they were beginning to shake. Baher was a good-looking man with very large hands. The way his hand covered her entire thigh made her feel feminine and definitely aroused. His hazel eyes were fixed on her and she immediately focused on them and then his lips. She licked her lip then held the bottom lip with her teeth.

"You've got great legs, Dani. They're long and sexy. I like this tattoo on your hip bone, a sunflower, very nice. Now let me see the bandage so I can fix it."

Van was immediately by her other side, and when she turned toward him to question him, Baher moved the towel out of the way.

She couldn't turn from Van's controlling stare, and it was too late when she realized her mistake in letting her guard down. Van placed his hand against her neck and face, and then moved in for a very intense kiss. His mouth devoured hers and they both began to duel over who was in control. Meanwhile, Baher moved both hands up the back of her thighs, his face was level with her pussy. She could feel his warm breath collide against her most sensitive flesh, and the towel, her safety blanket, was nowhere to be found.

Van continued to torment her mouth, licking, pulling, and then nibbling her lips and tongue before plunging into her mouth again and again. She absorbed every sensation, every bit of masculinity and commanding sense about him from his muscular chin to his possessive lips. She nearly jumped out of her skin when she felt Baher's lips against her folds then his tongue push against her pussy.

She moaned against Van's mouth and tried to retreat, but neither man would allow that. She gripped Van's shoulders for support as Baher lifted her thigh over his shoulder so he could gain better access to her body.

Every inch of her screamed with celebration and enjoyment. It had been so long since she was touched like this. As a matter of fact, nothing, no foreplay or even sex felt as hot and heavy and hopefully satisfying as she thought it might get. When he pressed a finger to her pussy, she pushed against Van and he held her firmly. The palm of his hand was plastered over her ass, pressing down as Baher thrust his finger into her pussy. He somehow brushed a digit between the crevice of her ass cheeks making her bend slightly so she could absorb every sensation. The two hard male bodies surrounding her added to her pleasure, and then Van cupped her right breast.

His hands were large, too, and her breasts felt full and her nipples hard from his ministrations. She felt everything to her core. From Van's calloused thumb caressing across her delicate nipple to Baher's digit moving in and out of her pussy. She wanted more. She wanted to throw inhibition to the wind and yell, "take me!"

As Baher added a second digit then licked against her folds, she exploded in pleasure, pulling her mouth from Van's in an attempt to catch her breath. Her head rolled back, and her hips thrust against Baher's fingers as she rode the amazing orgasm out.

She felt Baher's fingers slow down. Then his tongue joined them as Van licked and sucked along her neck. He pinched her nipple making her gasp then moan. It was an overload of emotions, sensations, and such an out-of-control reaction to two very intriguing strangers. She couldn't let this go any further. It wasn't right and she wasn't this easy.

"You have to stop. Oh God, this is so bad."

"You're very naughty, Daniella. You need discipline." Van teased her then squeezed her ass cheek hard while Baher pumped his fingers upward. Van's long, hard digit pressed between the crevice of her ass harder, causing pressure against her puckered hole, all while Baher continued to pump his digits into her pussy. She was stunned that she came.

"Oh!" She gasped in surprise but molded herself tighter against Van, but it was too hard, making herself jump from the pain in her side.

All touching ceased. Baher pulled his fingers slowly from her pussy then kissed her there. Van turned her toward Baher, lifting her right arm up and over her shoulder and placed it on his neck. Van used both hands to reach under her arms and cup her breast with one while the other kept her arm up and away from the bandages. If his controlling hold on her was meant to make her remain still, he was out of his fucking mind. She was tight as a spring in need of their touch, and she had come at least twice already.

She wanted Baher's fingers back inside of her, or better yet, his cock would be perfect. With her breasts pushed out all taut and nipples hard, her arm held upright as if she were bound to Van while her lower half dripped with need as Baher tended to her wound, she felt like screaming. In this position, she was fully exposed to Baher. He had to see her cream dripping down her thigh, and every time she tensed and tried to close her thighs, her body shook and her pussy quaked. It was them. It was these two men that did it to her.

She panted still, and she was suddenly embarrassed. She was acting like she'd never been touched by a sex god before. She watched the intensity on Baher's face.

Okay, so I've never met any sex gods before now.

She attempted to tighten her thighs together, but then Van pressed his thigh between them from behind her. The material of his pants was like an accelerant and enflamed her skin, making her feel ready to combust. She began to slightly move back and forth. Her pussy rubbed against the material until Van gripped her a little tighter, indicating her to stop.

Holy fuck, I'm gyrating against him.

His palm cupped her breast tighter then lowered down the swell of her belly, straight to her pussy where she needed it most. He used his fingers to spread her pussy lips as he whispered against her neck.

"I like you spread open like this." He took a deep breath of air. "I can smell your delicious cream, Daniella, and I want a taste as soon as Baher's done."

She closed her eyes and willed back her body's immediate reaction to Van's voice and words, but it was no use. She felt her cream drip.

"Let's take care of this." Baher's voice caught her off guard as she stirred beneath Van's ministrations. Baher slowly began to pull the tape and bandage from her moist skin. She cringed from the pinching pain but was so overly aroused that she would accept pain over the embarrassing emotions she had. She let two men touch her so intimately at the same time. As Baher pulled the sticky bandage from her sensitive skin, she felt aroused instead of any pain or pinching. How was that possible?

Baher moved slowly and Dani tried to control her breathing as the giant behind her alternated between playing with her breast and pussy, pinning one of her arms against his neck as he did so. The rough, heavy weight of his hand caressed along her skin, making her tense. As she absorbed the sensations she felt little spasms of release from her core. *How the hell is he doing that to me?* He moved his other hand away from her pussy, and she wanted to order him back but couldn't.

"Your health and safety are our top priorities, Daniella. Let Baher finish and then I'll take care of that hunger you feel inside of you," Van whispered as he pulled her nipple then licked across her neck.

"It's Dani," she stated firmly. It pissed her off, turned her on, and made her weak. She didn't do weak.

"I like to call you Daniella. Dani's a boy's name and you are no boy." Van pinched her nipple again and pressed the palm of his hand down her belly to her pussy, cupping it hard while his thigh pressed forward.

Her body rubbed against his jean-covered thigh, the sensation of hard muscle against soft tissue had her moaning, but then he pinched her just as Baher ripped the last strip of tape from her skin.

"Ouch," she moaned.

"Sorry, baby," Baher stated as she looked down at him. Van moved his hand off her pussy, and Baher kissed her pussy lips then licked between the folds.

She swallowed hard.

"I am so screwed," she whispered in defeat of their tactics.

"You will be shortly," Van whispered.

"No, that's not what I meant. God, you're driving me crazy and it's just not fair or right. I don't know either of you."

"But you will, and right now, your body knows that it wants us, Daniella. That is most important."

His words lingered in her mind as all titillation halted. She remained there between them, strung tight and fighting every sensation now after his professed words.

When she started to relax, realizing that it was no use fighting him when she was naked, he caressed her hip with his free hand and moved it upward until he caressed her breast and left his hand there as if he had every given right to do so. The warmth from his large hand penetrated fully, causing her heart rate to increase and a feeling of contentedness to consume her. There was also a burning sensation coming from the back of her neck against the hairline. It pricked and tickled down her spine.

She moaned and Baher continued.

"It's pretty red so we'd better add some ointment before I cover it." He began to squeeze some ointment onto his fingers and then gently added it to the stitching.

"You have a very tasty and pretty little pussy, Daniella. I can't wait to fuck this pussy." Van pressed the hand he had on her breast down her belly and to her mound. She found herself lifting her hips up and forward as he trailed a long, thick digit between her folds.

"Spread your legs for him, Dani. He's your Alpha," Baher told her, and she froze in place.

Why did those words turn her on? She was responding to "Alpha" as if she understood its significance.

Baher added the bandages and began to re-tape the wound when Van pressed his finger up into her channel.

"Oh," she moaned and pressed her ass back against him. She could feel his cock press hard against the crack of her ass, and crazy thoughts filled her mind. Sex with more than one man would require anal and oral sex. She could be living a fantasy with these guys.

"Spread them, Dani, now." Baher caressed her inner thigh, making her open wider.

"Oh damn!" she moaned and came again, dripping cream down her thighs.

"You are so responsive, baby. I love this body. It's perfect." Van nibbled her earlobe as he pumped his fingers a little faster.

She was riding his hand, and the feel of his hard knuckles colliding with her mound brought on an urge deep inside her. She was losing control. Van was a master when it came to a woman's body. He rubbed slowly, back and forth against her pubic bone as if he read her mind. She began to push back against him, the need for harder pressure was making her pump her hips. All of this was happening as Baher finished up dressing her cut. Over and over she moaned and pleaded for him to keep going, when finally she exploded again. Her body shook and then Baher fell to his knees, lifted her thigh up over his shoulder, and moved right in for a taste. His tongue collided with her very wet pussy and began to feast on her. She swayed and held his thick shoulders until he had his fill.

As her eyes popped open, she saw Randolph standing in the doorway and she tightened up.

Both Van and Baher didn't even look toward their brother.

"Dinner," he told them.

"Dessert's first tonight," Baher stated then chuckled as Van ran his teeth over Dani's neck. She squirmed and pleaded then released again.

She was a pile of mush and couldn't stand. She'd had it. She was exhausted.

* * * *

Randolph could smell Dani's delicious scent from the hallway. His heart pounded inside of his chest and his cock swelled, thick and hard beneath his camo pants. He walked into the bathroom, looking her body over. She was gorgeous, with large breasts and pretty pink nipples that looked like berries to pick and suck. He felt his eyes begin to glow slightly. Van was holding her, cupping one breast and rubbing his thumb gently over the nipple while he used his other hand to secure her arm above her head.

"Leave that up, you hear me?" Van warned Dani. She nodded, and he let his other hand slide down her arm, over her armpit, right to her other breast. His large hands now cupped both breasts. Randolph stared at her.

"Come take a taste of our sweet mate, Randolph," Baher stated after licking her cream and moving to the side.

Dani tried to press her thighs together and lower her arm as if embarrassed by her exposure.

"Don't!" both Randolph and Van stated, and she immediately placed her arm back up and over her head.

Randolph locked gazes with Dani. Her light-green eyes looked hazed over, her pupils dilated, and her full round lips parted.

He moved in front of her, maintaining eye contact.

He was an extra large man. Built with muscles upon muscles, and with all his tattoos, he knew he appeared intimidating. She looked delicate, feminine, yet everything inside him told him that Daniella was strong, maybe even to a fault. He didn't want his woman battling rogue wolves. He didn't like seeing her injured and covered in blood.

He lowered himself to his knees and she shook. He hoped it wasn't in fear.

"He won't hurt you," Van whispered then gave a look toward Randolph as if wanting him to say more to Dani to ease her mind. Well, he wasn't big on words, and right now, if he spoke, he'd say something stupid or too intense. Instead, he would show what her body did to him.

He touched her ankle and squeezed gently, his thumb and pinky touched one another with room to spare. He looked back up at her and she seemed to realize the same thing.

He lifted her leg and caressed his palm against her soft, feminine skin then leaned down to press his lips to her skin. She allowed him to bend her knee and place it over his shoulder while he used his palm to touch her.

"Like silk," he whispered, moving his digits slowly up her inner thigh and right to her pussy. As the tips of his fingers brushed against her sensitive flesh, she moaned.

She was panting and pressing her pussy forward. His eyes burned and his insides fought for control of his wolf. He wanted to bite her, claim her this second.

Instead, he pressed one long, thick digit between her delicate flesh.

"Oh God." She moaned and his digit wasn't even fully inside of her.

"Easy now," he whispered then pushed upward. Her pussy responded, lubricating his finger and allowing him better access to her. He pumped his finger upward and Baher caressed her other inner thigh, spreading her wider.

In and out he pumped his finger then couldn't hold off any longer. He needed to taste her.

He spoke to his brothers through their link and they helped prepare her body. He was a big man and needed room. He was nearly out of breath from squatting so low on the ground. Van lifted her up. He sat on the vanity and spread her legs over his thighs. Before she could decipher what was happening, Randolph was between her thighs inhaling her scent. His wolf eyes glowed, and he licked her then raised his eyes to see her face.

She watched in awe, her light-green eyes glazed over with arousal, and he let his wolf tongue show.

She gasped and he plunged it into her, rotating, caressing and devouring her cream as she exploded over and over again.

He used his hands to spread her pussy lips and then press his finger lower and under her. He continued to eat at her then pressed a digit against her puckered hole.

He pushed through. Her cream lubricated both entrances while he thrust tongue and finger into each.

She screamed and bucked on Van's lap as Randolph continued to bring her pleasure.

* * * *

"Oh please, I can't take it. Oh!" Dani screamed then fell back against Van's chest. Randolph was a giant, and he just brought her to climax while his finger had gone where no man had gone before.

As he pulled from her body, that magnificent, long wolf tongue licked her clean. How the hell did he do that? She wasn't turned off but utterly turned on.

"Is the party in here?" Miele asked as Bently followed him into the bathroom.

"No, no more, please, I can't take it," Dani stated, out of breath as Van massaged her breasts and Randolph kissed her inner thighs then lifted them off of Van. Randolph cupped her cheek and stared down at her. He looked so intense, and he was definitely a man of few words. But what he said to her as he played with her body turned her into a sex-craved lunatic. She swallowed hard.

He leaned down closer to her face.

"Perfect," he said then kissed her. He lifted her up, and she instinctively wrapped her arms around his neck as he carried her out of the bathroom, past Bently and Miele, and to the bed. He sat her down and the others joined them. Van pulled a T-shirt from the edge of the bed that was folded neatly along with a pair of boxers.

Randolph helped her into it, and before he released her, he gently caressed his knuckles against her cheek.

Oh God, I'm in love with a giant wolf.

"Let's get these on and go get dinner. You must be starving," Baher stated then tried to place her feet into the boxers. He lifted her by her waist and pulled them up.

"Thank you." She looked up at each of them.

They smiled except for Van and Randolph.

Randolph was in front of her again. He bent down and lifted her into his arms.

"Hold on," he told her firmly. She swallowed hard and wrapped her arms around his neck as he carried her out of the bedroom and down the stairs.

Chapter 7

Dani was sore. There was no denying that. This was the first time in her career, never mind her life, that she got injured like this. However, call her crazy, but she was feeling kind of on a high and numb around the Fagan men. It was so insane and there was this constant tingling, almost burning sensation on the back of her neck, just below the hairline. It felt as if an imaginary line extended down her spine and through her body, every part but especially her pussy and breasts.

She rubbed the back of her neck as she watched the five men that gathered around the large industrial-like kitchen, preparing dinner. The table was set, beer and wine being served as Miele added roasted chicken to a large white platter. He looked kind of sexy and domesticated. That made her chuckle to herself. It was hard to believe that these men could turn into wolves whenever they wanted to. She clutched her stomach and closed her eyes as she thought about the killer. She was scared. She was trying to be tough because she was a highly trained professional, in a profession and position as a homicide detective in New York City. She'd proven herself and her capabilities in the past, and this time would be no different.

"Are you feeling okay?" she heard Bently ask as he reached toward her face to gently push a loose strand of hair from her cheek.

He was a flirt and then some. She knew the type, except he also had that extra umph of something that made her pussy tingle just from his focus on her.

It was eerie and also interesting.

"I'm fine, thank you," she whispered then got that burning sensation at the base of her neck. She reached back and rubbed it.

"Hey, you keep doing that. Is your neck bothering you?" Baher asked as he reached toward her shoulders from behind and began to massage there. The tingling subsided. *How odd.*

She didn't want to tell them what she was feeling. As wild as it seemed that she trusted them, she didn't want to give in so easily. It was her stubborn, "I can take care of myself" attitude. She knew this. She wasn't denying her attraction to the men. That would be hopeless, but she didn't have to come off as easy. Like she did upstairs in their damn bathroom. She was ready to spread her legs and yell, "Orgy...who's in?"

She felt her cheeks warm. She needed more than sex from them. She felt it to the depths of her soul. She was standing her ground.

She wiggled off the stool, pushing Bently's hands off her shoulders and nearly knocking him out of the way. As she stood, she cringed with pain and took a few short, necessary breaths. Damn did that hurt, and now that she placed some distance between herself and the two men, she felt that burning sensation on her neck. *What the fuck!*

Miele placed the platter of chicken on the table as the others grabbed the side dishes of food. Bently and Baher stared at her then both reached for her chair to hold it out so she could sit. She felt a little guilty for pushing them away, but she needed to establish some boundaries. If they kept touching her, any of them, then she was as good as fucked, literally, and right now she needed her wits about her.

Dani was surprised when Bently moved around to the other side of the table, next to Van who sat directly across from her. Randolph sat on the other side of Van. She looked toward him, and he had his hands clasped together a few inches below his chin as his bold green eyes bore into her. Again, her body was in full awareness of these men.

Now Baher and Miele took position on either side of her. Their arms brushed against her arms, and she felt herself take a quick inhale of breath, then feel the perspiration hit her brow. She was so oversensitive she felt like one of those live wires knocked down during a thunder-and-lightning storm that danced along the blacktop, out of control. She was doing everything she could to ignore these sensations as she squeezed her thighs together

"Eat, Dani. I can hear your stomach growling from here," Van stated, his voice firm and authoritative, making her jump then stare at him. She was not used to being ordered around. They needed to understand that or they would fight all the time.

"Those are some intense wolf senses you have, Van, that you can hear my belly rumble from over there." She used the tongs to grab a juicy piece of roasted chicken, the aroma making her belly rumble louder this time.

"As wolves, we have extraordinary senses, especially the sense of smell and instinctive abilities," Van replied, taking a piece of chicken before adding a pile of potatoes to his plate. His brothers followed suit. They had let her take her food first, then the Alpha, interesting.

"What else can you sense right now with all this delicious food filling the air?" she asked, kind of egging him on or almost challenging this concept of innate abilities wolves supposedly had.

She was cutting her chicken and glanced up at Van and those gorgeous green eyes of his, waiting for a response from him. He looked her over and every body part came alive.

"I can smell your arousal, Daniella, and sense your need to fight those sensations running rampant in your body. I can smell your sweet cream and practically taste it on my tongue."

For the love of God, why, why did I antagonize this man?

She swallowed hard and tried not to falter at his stare. Her cheeks burned, and arousal filled her to the core. She noticed the others had a similar ability to stare deeply and almost expect others to lower their eyes and bow down, and it pissed her off that she felt that sensation now.

Dani put her shoulders back then forked a piece of chicken and brought it to her lips.

"Well, you've had a taste, Alpha, but it doesn't mean you'll get another." She took the piece of chicken and forced herself to chew and not choke on it as Van's eyes glowed, showing his wolf. He smirked then began to eat as if his non-retort and facial expression said it all. The pompous bastard knew she was fighting him on this, and he blew her off. Now that was a way to piss off a woman.

The silence continued as they ate their dinner. She was feeling much better after the delicious meal. She needed to start laying the groundwork for her departure from these men. She had work to do and needed to investigate the recent murders and how this killer knew she was headed to Baily's and why he killed Baily.

She wiped her mouth, took a sip of wine, then cleared her throat before placing her hands under her chin as Van had done earlier.

"So, gentleman, I appreciate your hospitality and all, but I do believe there is a killer running loose and I need to catch him. So if you could get me my clothes, I'll get out of your hair, no pun intended, and hit the road." She began to get up.

"Sit, Daniella," Van barked, and she froze as the others began to rise from their seats and clear the table. No one looked at her, not even Randolph.

"You will remain under our protection, Daniella. You are our mate, our responsibility, and life as you know must change."

He stood up as if he were dismissing any attempt from her to retort or have a say in her life. And what was with this mating bullshit?

"Van, I don't know what the hell you're talking about, but my life is not going to change. I have an apartment, a career, and a responsibility to this community to find this piece of crap, and I intend on doing it." She rose from the table.

"No, Daniella, you are not. You are the mate of wolves, and this conversation is finished."

"Bullshit!" she yelled and slammed her fist down on the table.

Van turned toward her with a mean gleam in his eyes, and the others stared at her, too, arms crossed in front of their chests. She felt the wind knocked out of her sails, as if she would fall over from the power emitting from them.

That damn burning hit her neck again, too, and it really hurt.

She reached back, holding the spot where it burned as the turmoil filled her belly. Every part of her wanted to be with these men. She wanted to have sex with them, cuddle with them, absorb their scents, and be part of them while the other part of her sought justice and wanted to maintain her independence. She was fighting more than just her personality and what she was used to. She was fighting something intangible, strong, and unidentifiable, but she knew it was there, deep inside of her.

"I am trying my hardest to be patient with you, Daniella."

"Dani! For crying out loud, my fucking name is Dani." She turned to leave only to grab her side and then her neck as the pain hit her. She gasped, and immediately Bently and Baher were by her side, helping her to sit back down.

"I don't want to sit back down. I will not be your prisoner. Damn it, you cannot do this to me, Van. My career is all I've got." Her heart filled with emotions. She was angry, scared, and confused about the instant attraction to five men who could shift into wolves. She was losing her mind, and the day's events were kicking in, making her feel shitty and defeated. She was tired, and with each step she took away from the men, the more exhausted she felt. *What the hell is wrong with me?*

Bently placed his hand under her chin and stared down at her. She felt the sincerity and depth of emotions from his brown eyes. It was a total contrast to Van's mean and aggressive behavior and tone.

"You are no longer alone, Dani. We are yours for eternity." He leaned down and kissed her lips softly. When their lips parted, she felt the pain in her neck ease. It was as if every time she tried to put some distance between herself and the Fagan men, she had that burning pain. She reached back and rubbed her neck.

"You're in pain still," Baher stated, standing next to her as he moved her hair off her shoulder away from her cheek.

"Miele, can you get one of those painkillers Charlie left for her?"

She heard the shaking of a pill container, and she wasn't sure that she wanted them.

"I don't want them. I don't know how they'll make me feel and I need to stay awake. I don't know any of you. I don't like feeling this out of control," she admitted as she glanced around the room.

Bently placed both hands on her cheeks and held her face gently between his hands as he stared down at her. Bently, the sexy flirt, with his sparkling brown eyes somehow seemed to calm her.

"Please trust us, Dani. We know what we're doing and we want to take care of you."

Miele appeared with a glass of water and one pill. Miele, always on the go, always keeping busy and ready to jump into action to assist. He was a doer. She just sensed that about him.

"Take this. Charlie said it may make you feel drowsy, but it will take away the pain."

She took the pill, hoping that it would in fact numb the pain in her side and in her neck but not make her fall asleep again. She had to be imagining things. There was no way that her body felt pain from being away from the men or placing some distance between them. How could that be? Did they do something to her while she was sleeping?

"Did you give me something earlier?" she asked without thinking it through.

Van raised his voice.

"Damn it, we don't go around drugging women, Daniella. Accept what you are feeling. It is your destiny."

God damn it to hell, I want to slug him right now. Destiny my ass! This is all a bad fucking nightmare.

She needed realty. She needed her life back.

Perhaps a change of subject would work here.

"I want to know what information you have on this killer. You have insight into his abilities and resources that I don't have." She looked toward Van.

He eyed her over.

"You need rest, Daniella. We can discuss this tomorrow."

With that dismissal, Van walked closer toward her and was about to pick her up. She was beginning to feel numb again and that sensation in her neck eased to a humming as Van reached for her.

"I'm not tired, Van. I need to know," she told him as he lifted her up into his arms. She immediately placed her arms around his neck.

Their faces were inches apart. Her entire body was alive with a sexual pull so intense she thought she might hyperventilate, never mind attack the man and rip his clothes off of his amazing body. *Yikes!*

"Tomorrow, Daniella, you will feel better and then we will discuss the future."

She didn't like his smug, controlling attitude, but her pussy sure did as it clenched and, damn it, moistened with arousal. He inhaled and his eyes glowed.

"You'll learn to listen to your body and your gut, Daniella."

He carried her out of the room, his words lingering in her head along with the drugs and Margo's same advice to follow her gut.

By the time they reached the bedroom, her head was against his shoulder and her eyes were heavy with exhaustion. But worst of all was the feeling of contentedness she felt in Van's arms.

Van placed her down on the bed then covered her with the sheets.

He brushed her hair from her cheeks as he leaned over her.

She held his gaze.

"You can't keep me drugged up, Alpha. It's not right and it isn't fair. I like to be in control, too," she whispered then blinked her eyes, trying to fight the need to close them and sleep.

He touched her cheek and caressed her lower lip with his thumb.

"We'll see about that, mate," he whispered.

The last thing she saw was his glowing green eyes. Then the feel of his lips pressed gently against her lips.

* * * *

"So what do you think?" Bently asked his brothers as they gathered around the kitchen.

"I think she's stubborn, independent, and used to handling shit on her own. You read her files and heard her commander's reports on her. She's tough, more than capable of handling herself, and good at her job," Baher stated.

"I don't want her chasing killers of any kind, never mind this rogue wolf who seems very interested in her," Miele added.

"I agree. She doesn't know much about wolves or their abilities to kill. What if he seeks her out to mate her? That scent she has is so enticing, and apparently we aren't the only ones who sense it," Baher stated.

"She's going to be learning a lot about wolves shortly. The same goes for being mated to us. The sooner we mark her and claim her as our mate, the safer she will be," Van stated as he entered the room.

"How is she, Van?" Bently asked.

"She is sleeping. Fought me until she passed out," he stated, and the others chuckled.

Van turned around to face them with a scowl on his face. Bently stared at his oldest brother.

"She does not bow down to anyone, and none of us are used to that," Bently pointed out.

"Well, she is going to learn just as we are going to learn how to handle being mated to such a woman," Van replied, and another set of chuckles went through the room.

"I, for one, think of it as an exciting challenge. She is too tasty of a morsel to resist," Bently replied.

"I think she will find submission most pleasurable in bed," Miele teased.

"I would still like to know what power she seems to possess to have such a keen scent about her. I'd like to speak with her friend Margo again. Perhaps the healer can enlighten us on our new mate," Van stated.

"I do not want Dani to leave our protection at all, but it seems inevitable. She does have a job to do and she enjoys it," Baher stated.

"She cannot be left unattended to. She is our mate and we need to watch over her. If she insists upon continuing in such a profession, then she will do it in Texas where she is protected by the packs," Van stated firmly.

"This is going to be hell," Baher added.

Just then, Van's cell phone rang, interrupting their conversation. The others listened with their ability to hear both sides of the conversation.

A few minutes later Van disconnected the call.

* * * *

"So, you all heard. It is becoming apparent that this wolf is not really a total wolf at all but perhaps a freak experiment gone badly," Van stated.

"That is fucked up and totally unreal. Who would have the ability to create such a beast?" Baher asked.

"I don't know but we will find out. You heard Zespian and he believes that this wolf was crossbred with something else," Van added.

"Its need to kill so violently and leave the scenes so bloody is sickening but may also be a clue," Miele stated.

"How so? What are you thinking, Miele?" Bently asked.

"Well, if what Zespian says is true, then perhaps when this wolf was created, it was crossed with something that craves blood."

"Damn, that could also explain its interest in Dani if her blood is as appealing as her scent. Her blood and scent contain something that we all can identify with, yet we know it is beyond the fact that she is our mate," Bently stated.

"She needs us," Randolph said, making everyone pause to look at him. They nodded their heads as Randolph walked out of the room. Van knew he was heading toward Dani's room to stay with her.

"We need to make some concrete plan here. Perhaps explaining the situation to Dani will help her see the seriousness of the case?" Miele suggested.

"I agree. She knows about investigation and the process. She'll want to continue, and we won't be able to stop her, but we can protect her while she is doing it," Bently added.

"I think mating her and marking her as our mate will help to seal the bond and protect her, too. Perhaps that alone will deter this rogue wolf from seeking what is ours," Van stated firmly. He was feeling uneasy and defensive. He knew he needed to be with Daniella, but she wasn't ready to submit, at least not without some major persuasion.

"I think we do need to persuade her, Van. She was quite responsive in the bathroom earlier. She wants us, she feels the desire and attraction, but we need to lead her. It is our duty and the way things are done," Baher told Van.

"Agreed," Van stated and the others made the same remarks.

"We will work on it as soon as she awakens." Van walked out of the kitchen.

Chapter 8

"We need to find him. At this rate, the Special Investigations Unit will catch on to my plans and destroy everything. Detrix has lost complete control of himself," Dr. Evans stated to his small committee.

"We knew he was going to be trouble from the start. Knowing Vanderlan and how powerful of a vampire he is, he probably tainted the blood we stole from his vault," Marfur Cartright stated. He was a commander for Dismar, an elder of the circle.

"You may be right. We thought by going to his place while he was away serving the Valdamar Packs that we could get away with it." Dr. Evans shook his head.

"What's done is done. We now need to find Detrix," Lemlock Porter, a scientist from London, added.

"My sources tell me that he is in New York. He has murdered over a dozen people. Apparently, one got away and that would be the one for us to seek out," Evans stated.

"Why do you say that? Who is it?" Marfur asked.

"I do not know yet. But whoever they are, we must get to them first and use them to bait in Detrix. Unless he gets to them before we can identify them." They all felt on edge and worried.

"Any word on the Unit becoming interested in these murders?" Lemlock asked.

"They are a tight-knit community of wolves. No one except those of great influence or power are privy to information. So the only way we will know if the Special Investigations Unit is on to these murders is if we see them or smell them around."

"Great. Well, let's hope your men find Detrix or this other person and fast. We've got another set of injections being administered to the other hybrid wolf. He is much larger than Detrix, faster, stronger, and a hell of a lot brighter, even without the vampire blood. He has been trained to know his purpose. If all goes according to plan, then my Alpha and elder in the circle, Dismar, can gain the power and control of Fagan Pack territory, bringing his numbers significantly higher. It is something he has been working on for quite some time," Marfur Cartright stated.

"It will be beneficial to all of us if Dismar gains greater power." Lemlock rose from the chair.

"Great. I am looking forward to seeing the newest hybrid in a bit. I have been quite impressed thus far, Lemlock. He is beyond Alpha material. He will rule beautifully. And how about the others? Will it be easier to form a small army of these rogues if their assistance is necessary?" Dr. Evans asked.

"Definitely. However, this rogue that I am calling 'the enforcer' will be successful alone." Porter stated.

"Wonderful and I am truly impressed. Perhaps we will be able to celebrate even sooner." Marfur added with a smile as he began to exit the room.

* * * *

Dani began to awaken as she felt the large, warm body that was pressed against her back. Her eyes were still heavy from the painkillers she had taken, but at least her side where the stitches were didn't hurt.

She felt the heavy hand across her belly and the gentle way his fingers brushed over her exposed skin. She wondered which one of the men was holding her and guessed by the size and scent of surrounding her that it was Randolph. He was huge and the largest of the Fagan brothers and equally as intimidating as Van.

She suddenly felt keenly aware of the man's size and heaviness of his hand. His fingers were thick and long, and her belly felt hot where it lay.

Her shirt must have lifted up as she slept, revealing her belly. Her insides tightened. *Fuck, I hope I don't look fat.*

Dani was always self-conscious about her weight and the little rounded belly she just couldn't seem to get rid of. She swallowed again, and the body behind her shifted. Instantly, she felt the long, thick object against her ass, making her insides burn with need. Her pussy clenched and her lips parted. The man was well built. He caressed her belly, moving his hand across her rib cage and now to her breast. But he didn't touch it, he just grazed fingertips across the under part making her wiggle. She knew that the Fagan brother behind her was Randolph. Any of the others would have spoken to her by now. He was definitely the quiet type but also very lethal.

She didn't want to acknowledge the effect he was having on her. She imagined his face in her mind as he continued to tease her skin. He was tough with dark hair and eyes that were nearly identical to the darkness of the strands of hair. He was covered with tattoos that stretched across and around each ridge of muscle on his weight-lifting body. She wondered if all wolves were so naturally fit and muscular, or perhaps they had very fast metabolisms. That was something she would love to have, a fast metabolism.

He took that moment to move his fingers higher and against her breast, the tip of his nail traced over the top of her nipple.

"Oh." She moaned as he continued to massage her breast.

She felt his lips against her shoulder and neck. The tingling sensation filled her, and she parted her legs then rubbed her thighs slowly together to try to stop the hunger building there.

Immediately his hand moved off her breast, down her ribs, and to her pussy that he cupped above the material of the boxers she wore. She tightened up, and he kissed her shoulder and her neck then rubbed a finger back and forth across her mound, spreading the material and her pussy lips.

"Open for me," he whispered, shocking her. She was surprised by the sudden sound of his voice almost as much as how quickly she parted her legs on Randolph's command.

She rolled to her back, and she looked into his eyes, dark, shiny and oh so sexy staring back at her.

They held one another's gaze as Randolph used his one hand to push her boxers down and off of her as she assisted. He remained staring into her eyes as he stroked a finger over her wet pussy. His expression hardened, his muscles in his shoulders tightened, and the need for him to be inside of her overwhelmed her senses.

Her lips parted and she took unsteady breaths as he began to press a digit up into her. As he breached her opening, she tilted her head back, losing the ability to hold his gaze as he pushed into her.

"Beautiful," he whispered then continued to stroke her pussy, pressing his digit in and out of her as he adjusted his position on the bed.

"Look at me, Daniella," Randolph stated, and she opened her eyes to stare at him.

He added a second digit after the next stroke, and she lifted her legs so he could gain better access.

"I want to taste you," he told her, and oh for crying out loud did he sound so fucking sexy. She nodded her head like an idiot instead of a strong female who knew about sex. However, her gut instincts were screaming that she didn't know shit about sex and that Randolph and his brothers wanted to teach her.

He began to move over her then between her legs. Before she could decipher his intentions, because she was in a dead staring contest with him, he lowered his head and his mouth latched onto her pussy.

He used the palms of his hands to spread her thighs as he ate at her, licking, sucking, and pulling at her sensitive flesh until she lost it.

"Randolph!" she said his name.

Her chest rose and fell in what she thought was an awkward manner as she locked gazes with Randolph. His dark eyes glimmered and shined like nothing she had ever seen before. They mesmerized her as he kissed her skin from mound to breasts to mouth.

She tasted herself on his lips, and as he plunged his tongue through her parted lips, she melted against his body.

Her legs were parted, spread by his large, thick thighs of steel covered in camo pants.

He released her lips only to breathe then went back for more as if he couldn't get enough of her lips. She had never felt so sexy and attractive. It was a wild thought that she became putty in this man's hands. He was a man who said few words but whose actions spoke in volumes.

Randolph lightened his strokes using his lips and teeth to nibble gently over her lips, down to her chin and over her neck.

She lifted her neck toward him, uncertain where the sensations were coming from. Flashes exploded inside her head with visions of him biting her. She never heard of any such thing until Margo explained a bit about wolves and mates. *But I am human. Where are these thoughts coming from?*

She gripped his shoulders best she could. "Randolph, please. This is going too fast."

He thrust his hips gently against her sensitive mound, and she gasped.

"Fast is good. I want you, Daniella. Now."

His demand was strong, yet he appeared needy, almost weak with desire. Perhaps she was wrong, but thus far she had seemed right on target with these men's intentions and control issues. This was something more. This was pure need. He was feeling exactly what she was feeling. She wanted him inside of her. She wanted to touch every inch of him and give him some bites of her own. She shocked herself when the words left her lips.

"I know, Randolph. I feel so alive with you. I'm scared but I want you."

He leaned down to kiss her lips softly then released them as he stood up and got off the bed.

She felt disappointment to the extreme when he left her body, her bed, but then he reached for the zipper of his pants, and her heart nearly did a somersault. He was a god, a gorgeous, wild, tattooed god with the biggest dick she had ever had the pleasure of seeing.

Her mouth dropped, and her expression brought pleasure and a smirk to Randolph's face.

"You're perfect." He leaped between her legs, spread her thighs, and lined his cock up against her pussy.

"This is forever. Tonight our union begins."

She nodded her head. She couldn't speak. She was too in awe of this man and the power that emanated from him. It was official. She was in lust with him.

Slowly he began to press forward, inch by inch, his thick, long cock filled her up, and she knew that she would never be the same woman again. Her emotions made her nearly choke up and cry. She felt every sensation, every touch, every stroke deep inside of her, and, damn it, that spot on the back of her neck felt at ease.

* * * *

Randolph's brothers spoke to him through their mind link and encouraged him to continue. This was a step in the right direction.

He absorbed her scent that was now all consuming. He urged his wolf to remain calm. Dani was his now. She would be bound to him and his brothers by morning.

"So tight and sweet. You feel so good," he whispered then locked his fingers through Dani's as he pressed them to either side of her head. He thrust his hips slowly, and she lifted up toward him, wanting him to penetrate deeper. But he knew if he let himself go, he wouldn't stop. He would claim her fully by biting into her shoulder to get a taste of her sweetness.

"That feels so good," she told him, and he looked down at her, in awe of his mate. She was beautiful, with muscular shoulders and arms, firm and built, not skin and bones. Her breasts were more than a handful and silky soft. He watched them bob and sway with every thrust he made.

He licked his lips, felt his wolf begin to surface.

"You're so big, Randolph. God, it feels so good."

He increased his speed, penetrating her more deeply with each thrust of his hips. He stared down at her. Her eyes were closed, her breasts lifted high as he remained holding her hands above her head now while he thrust and rotated his hips.

"So tight and wet for me, Dani. Look at me, mate."

Her eyes popped open, and he hid his chuckle. She really was going to fight them tooth and nail on this. Well, not if he had anything to say about it.

He thrust again and again until he set a steady, fast rhythm that made Dani close her eyes and moan.

"Look at me, Dani," he demanded of her, and immediately she opened her eyes. He pulled out to the tip of his cock then shoved in fast.

"Oh!" She gasped and he did the same thing again and again until he felt his wolf come close to the surface. It chanted him on, made him want to finalize this act of lovemaking with his mate.

"Fuck, Dani, I can't hold off."

He rocked into her, causing the bed to creak and moan from his deep, fast strokes. He felt Dani's heels dig into his back and she began calling his name and turning her head side to side. He thrust one final time and held himself inside of her as he exploded then bit into her neck.

He tasted her blood. It stung his tongue and oozed down his throat. He felt weak and then came the numbing pain before he pulled from her and fell to the side.

* * * *

Dani tried to catch her breath and then she noticed how quickly Randolph had pulled from her body. Had it just been sex for him after all? Her shoulder burned and when she looked to where he had bitten her, she saw her own flesh smooth over and destroy the bite mark. *What the hell?*

Then she heard him moan just as the bedroom door slammed open and his brothers entered, looking worried and pissed off.

"What the fuck did you do to him?" Van demanded to know.

"I didn't do anything," Dani began to say as she pulled the shirt up off the bed and covered herself best she could.

Randolph moaned and she reached for him to caress his skin.

"What's wrong with him?" she asked as his brothers tended to him. As Bently and Baher approached Randolph, a scent of some sort must have hit them hard because each made a funny noise and covered their mouths and noses as they stepped back away from her.

"It can't be. There's no fucking way," Bently stated aloud as he stared at Dani.

"What? What's going on, please talk to me."

She began to shake, not knowing what had happened but feeling that she was completely at fault for Randolph's current state.

An odd sensation began to fill her.

They looked at Randolph. He held their gaze and it appeared as if some sort of private communication was occurring between them.

"You truly do not know what is happening here?" Bently asked. His brown eyes filled with concern.

She shook her head and Miele took her hand.

"Maybe I should take her out of the room, and then you can make the call, Van," Miele suggested.

"No. She stays," Randolph spoke. His voice sounded distorted and rough.

"I will make the call. Stay with them." Van looked at her one last time before exiting the room.

* * * *

They allowed her to shower and get dressed in another one of their borrowed T-shirts and boxers. Randolph was still feeling weak, and of course being a man of few words, he hadn't said much to her. The overlarge wolf did pull her into his arms and hold her tight. She needed it, and she was rather taken aback by his need for cuddling.

His warm breath caressed her neck and his arm wrapped around her waist like a vise grip, as her mind absorbed what it could.

Her thoughts wandered back to her conversation with Margo. She had seemed amazed at the way that star necklace shined in purple. It was as if that wasn't supposed to happen. Of course that was just a gut instinct on Dani's part, but still she felt her mind leaning toward believing that had something to do with what happened between herself and Randolph.

Randolph gave her a squeeze every few moments making her heart race and a burning sensation fill her. Tears stung her eyes. She wouldn't hurt Randolph or the others for anything. She was confused.

* * * *

"Margo will be here soon," Van told his brothers as they joined together in the living room.

The sound of the doorbell ringing brought Bently to his feet as he made his way to the center hall to answer it.

"What in the world are you doing here?" Bently asked as Vanderlan, a vampire they knew all too well stood on their doorstep.

"Where is she?" Vanderlan asked with authority and attitude. It was his usual demeanor that tended to make many falter or show fear. Bently was an Alpha wolf just like his brothers. They didn't back down from anyone. Especially not vampires. They considered Vanderlan a friend.

Was Vanderlan speaking of Dani? Suddenly Bently's hackles rose and his brothers immediately joined him in the front entranceway.

"Who do you mean when you ask where is she?" Bently asked.

"The one who calls to me. A woman who shares my blood."

Chapter 9

Van opened the bedroom door. He was fighting every declaration of his wolf to protect her from the bloodletter. Truth was, they had no idea who or what Dani was. Vanderlan was a very influential and widely known vampire. They had worked together many times over the years. He was considered a friend amongst many of the were packs, and to the Fagan Pack, they considered him even closer. They had worked together over the century to protect the circle of elders, the sanctity of the supernatural, and the humans from rogues of every kind. Lately, it seemed as if there were more rogues emerging every day. Just a few months back they had captured and killed a rabid shifter. The urge to kill turned him into a serial killer.

They needed to get to the bottom of this situation. How could Dani share Vanderlan's blood and what did it mean?

"Dani, you are needed downstairs," Van commanded.

She looked surprised and began to move when Randolph pulled her back against him and snuggled close to her neck.

"She stays."

Van sent his thoughts to Randolph, making him understand the seriousness of the situation and who was standing, waiting downstairs in the living room.

Randolph sat up.

"No. She will not see him."

"She must see him. We have to get to the bottom of this. She could have killed you or all of us."

"What? What are you two talking about?" Dani asked.

"We must go downstairs now. Come." Van moved toward the bed and reached his hand out for her to take it. She hesitated, looking at Randolph for approval. It made Van feel a bit jealous, but the positive was that she was bonding with at least one of them. It was a start. They weren't giving Dani up to anyone.

* * * *

Dani had no idea what was going on, but as she walked down the stairs and glanced into the living room she immediately noticed a stranger amongst the other Fagan brothers. He was tall, at least six and a half feet and had black hair and piercing black eyes. He locked gazes with her, and she released Randolph's hand and froze in place.

His eyes began to glow red. Was that even possible? What was he?

She felt a pull of some sort. It was way different than what she felt for the brothers. It was a connection of sorts deep within her body, her blood. Yeah, she felt it pump through her veins. Somehow she knew this man.

"I'm sorry, but do I know you?" she asked, and with no recollection as to why or how she got there, she was suddenly inches from his body and staring up into his eyes. She heard the low growls around her, but she was too hypnotized by the gorgeous man above her with the red, glowing eyes.

He was dressed all in black, his attire reeked of high class and money. He reached toward her face, and when his fingers touched her skin, they were very cold yet gentle. She noticed the ruby red and gold ring on his pinky and the color of his skin. He was tan and appeared as if he had been sunbathing recently.

"Dani, this is Vanderlan. He is a vampire," Van stated from beside her, and she had difficulty registering his words. *Did he just say vampire?*

She slowly turned away from Vanderlan, feeling a hold or something trying to make her remain staring at him, but her own decision to look toward Van overpowered it.

Vanderlan chuckled.

"You're joking right?" she asked Van, and Van shook his head.

She looked back toward Vanderlan. He was smirking.

"You are an exceptional creature. Your powers are great, Daniella, and a blessing.

"I came here with great concern that I would be forced to kill the mate of five good, Alpha men, but it seems that fate has decided something entirely different."

"You're not really a vampire are you?" she asked. The man was tan for Christ's sake, and it was the middle of the damn day. Didn't vampires have to remain in the dark and stay out of the sun? *What am I thinking? Vampires are not real!*

"I can sense your confusion, Daniella. Let me explain. Come sit with me," Vanderlan stated then took her hand and led her toward the couch. The others were still nearby and they didn't seem too happy either.

"I am a vampire. They do exist. I, however, have the ability to remain in the sunlight thanks to a very close friend of mine. But that is another story for another day. What I would like to know is where you came from and how you have my blood within you? It has been flowing through you since birth, which can only mean that one of your parents, is a descendant of mine. Can you tell me who they are?"

She shook her head, and he looked upset. She felt compelled to help him. It was so strange but she really got the impression that he was good and they could be friends. *So freaking crazy. Me, friends with a vampire? Well, it was just as crazy as me sleeping with a wolf and ready and willing to sleep with four other wolves who also happen to be brothers.*

"I'm sorry, Vanderlan, I do not know who my biological parents are. I was adopted."

Just then the doorbell rang, and Bently went to answer it.

"Perhaps that is Margo," Miele suggested, and Dani thought he sounded hopeful. They had called Margo over. What in the world was going on here?

Dani turned to look at Margo, but she felt Vanderlan's eyes upon her and then his hand clasped hers tightly.

"Must you hold her hand like that?" Randolph asked, making Dani jump.

"Yes," the vamp stated without even looking at Randolph. Vanderlan was just as commanding and controlling as the wolves.

Dani froze in her position as she felt the tiny warm tingling sensation travel from where their hands locked straight up her arm. As it traveled along her breast, she flinched and giggled slightly.

"Are you doing that?" she asked Vanderlan, and he kept his expression blank, but his eyes glowed red. She suddenly felt a sexual pull toward the vampire. It was so crazy. How could this possibly be happening to her? She was a freak. A sex-craved freak wanting to spread her legs for every sexy, good-looking man in her presence, despite the fact that none of them were even human.

"Oh God, Dani, I was so worried about you," Margo interrupted as she came practically running into the room, but before she reached Dani, Margo stopped short. Her eyes locked gazes with Vanderlan, and then she bowed before lowering to one knee.

"Oh shit, this is not good," Dani stated aloud, and Vanderlan laughed then squeezed her hand.

"Margo, please stand. I thank you for your public show of respect, honey. I see we have ourselves quite the situation. Perhaps you may be able to clear the air?" Vanderlan asked, and Margo stood up and blushed as she looked at the vampire. Dani chuckled. Margo had good taste. That was for sure.

"She is special, sir. She is a healer," Margo stated, and multiple responses and gasps of surprise traveled through the room. The only one who seemed somewhat calm was Vanderlan.

"I see. Who are her parents?" Vanderlan asked, and Dani stared at them.

"You know who my parents are?" Dani asked, pulling from Vanderlan and standing up.

"I am not certain, Dani. I swear this to you. All I know is that you are a healer and your destiny lies with the Fagan Pack."

"She's a healer? Then why after she had sex with Randolph and he bit her was he in massive pain, and her wound instantly healed?" Baher asked.

Dani was shocked at the blatant way they spoke of her and Randolph having sex. She was shy and embarrassed as she lowered her head.

"She has always had the power to heal, but until she finds her mates and seals the bond, she can't heal her own wounds. You see, as far as we know, she is one of a kind. I am assuming that you, Vanderlan, are the vampire whose blood she shares?" Margo asked, and Vanderlan nodded his head.

"How did that happen?" Dani asked, surprised that she was even asking coherent questions.

"Not sure, really. The vamp would be the one to know. At some point, Vanderlan, you exchanged blood with a wolf or wolves. I believe that then one of those wolves mated and they had a child, that is, Dani. Then something must have happened to them. Wolves do not leave their babies for anything," Margo explained.

"Hold the phone! Wait one darn minute. You're serious. You're saying that not only do I have vampire blood in me but also wolf blood?"

"Holy shit," Miele stated.

"That's an understatement. That's just far out and no. No, I am not either. You are all fucking crazy!" Dani began to walk away when Vanderlan grabbed her hand.

Van was immediately against her back, his arm wrapped around her waist. Vanderlan began to breathe deeply and so did Van.

Something primal and animalistic was happening here. She felt it engulf her body. Her neck burned uncontrollably and the star necklace was glowing bright.

"Holy shit!" Margo exclaimed.

Dani shook. She was wedged between Vanderlan and Van. Their massive, hard bodies aroused every inch of her.

She closed her eyes and embraced the feelings consuming her.

"This just got very complicated," Vanderlan stated.

"Not happening vamp," Van responded.

"No fucking way," Randolph added, and then Bently, Miele, and Baher surrounded the three of them. The moment they all touched, Dani moaned as she felt the burning against the back of her neck cause massive pain. The star necklace fell from her neck and suddenly the room spun and she was engulfed in darkness.

* * * *

"What the hell was that?" Van demanded to know as Vanderlan lifted Dani up into his arms and against his shoulder.

"You felt that?" Vanderlan asked, appearing surprised.

"I think we all did," Miele added.

"She was in pain a moment, and she grabbed her neck," Bently stated.

"She's been doing that a lot lately," Baher added.

Vanderlan lifted her a little higher against him. He knew this was an odd arrangement by the gods, but it was their destiny. He pushed her long, brown locks away from her face.

"Van, lift her hair up so they can see her neck."

"Oh God, her necklace broke. This isn't good," Margo stated as she bent down to pick up the chain.

"What is this?" Van stated aloud as the others spotted what he was staring at.

"Is the mark on her neck wolf?" Vanderlan asked, knowing that it would be. She was the one he had waited for.

"It looks like a tattoo of a star but it is purple like the color of violets," Van stated.

"She will be okay. The bond will take and we will work this all out. Somehow, we'll work this out," Vanderlan told them, and he squeezed Dani against his body and inhaled her scent.

"Give her to me now. She is our mate, and we will care for her." Bently reached for Dani.

Vanderlan turned away.

"We will care for her together, wolf. She belongs to me as well."

* * * *

"So let me get this straight, you are telling us that Daniella is not only our mate but also yours?" Van asked as his incisors elongated. He was fighting his wolf just as his brothers were fighting their own.

Vanderlan nodded his head as he held Van's gaze. The vamp's legs were crossed as he leaned back into the single recliner, looking quite content. Van and his brothers, on the other hand, wanted to rip his fucking head off. A fucking vamp was mate to their mate? How the hell was that supposed to work? It wasn't even heard of before.

He felt the slight uneasiness in his head and then a calming tone. At first Van leaned toward it as support and then reality hit him. He looked at Vanderlan.

"Get out of my head, bloodletter!" Van yelled then stood up and began to pace. Vanderlan remained reclined in the seat while Van's brothers looked on the defensive.

"I mean no harm, wolf. I was trying to help you."

"I don't need your help. What my brothers and I need is for you to leave here."

"That is not going to happen." Vanderlan glanced toward the bedroom door.

It had been an hour since the incident downstairs. Margo had tried to offer some advice, but this situation was shocking, even to her, and unheard of.

Margo wanted to remain by Daniella's side, but Vanderlan had refused her and so did the others. Instead, they sent her home and told her that they would contact her tomorrow if necessary.

"Tell us how you know that Daniella is your mate, too?" Van asked and Randolph growled low. Vanderlan looked at him with confidence and control.

"I am trying to remember when it was that I bit her relative. I would have to taste her blood myself to be sure when, but she seems strong. I thought I was after someone else."

"You are not tasting her blood," Randolph interjected.

"It will happen, Randolph. She will find much pleasure in it. I assure you."

"Fuck that!" Bently yelled and stood up, prepared to fight.

"We could exchange blows over this or we could face the reality of the situation. There is more I need to tell you. While Daniella sleeps, I will explain how I located her."

"She's twenty-six years old. Why would it take this long for you to find her?" Miele asked Vanderlan.

"I was not searching for her, Miele. As you know, I have been busy working various cases for many packs related to you. Your pack in particular, as you should recall, has been under attack by rogues for quite some time."

"Rogues follow all the packs and try to infiltrate them," Baher replied on the defensive.

"That may be true, but your packs have been infiltrated more often than not. Also remember that you are one of the smaller packs."

"We may be smaller than most, but we still rule what is ours. We will not be overtaken," Van stated in a fierce voice.

"That is good to know, but it appears you may need some help."

"Not from a bloodletter," Randolph stated.

Vanderlan raised his eyebrow at Randolph.

"Fate has already stepped in, my friend. It appears that we will be getting to know one another very well."

Miele stood up and began to pace.

"I don't get it. Why? What seems to be the reasoning behind this?" Miele asked.

"There is a situation we need to discuss. I believe that our woman has been trying to capture a killer believed to be of the wolf."

Van did not like the way Vanderlan was calling he and his brothers' Daniella "our woman" as if he was included in this mating. But then Vanderlan's words sunk in.

"You know of this killer? The one that seeks her out?" Van asked.

Vanderlan leaned forward in his chair.

"He seeks her out? He's seen her?"

"She escaped the first time on her own, and the second time just barely, which is how she landed here under our care and protection," Van stated.

"He cannot have her. Son of a bitch!" Vanderlan yelled and rose from his chair.

"Do you know who it is? Have you gotten any leads?" Vanderlan asked, appearing quite upset.

"None yet. Zespian called us in on the case, hoping that we would intervene and capture this wolf before he could do more damage," Bently stated.

"Zespian is your uncle, correct?"

Van nodded.

Vanderlan release a short sigh then shook his head.

"Your uncle and I go way back. Does he know that Daniella is your mate?"

"Yes. We informed him last night so that we could get another team to continue the investigation and figure out where the rogue wolf is hiding," Miele added.

"I will be sure to speak with him. In the meantime, we need to work out a schedule of sorts to watch over our mate. She will not be allowed anymore involvement in this investigation," Vanderlan stated firmly.

"Bullshit I won't," Dani stated as she crossed her arms in front of her chest and stared at Vanderlan.

* * * *

Dani had heard quite enough information from Vanderlan. As sexually aroused as she felt, she knew she needed to calm down and straighten this situation out. These men were not like human men.

"Daniella, how are you feeling?" Miele asked as he assisted her by taking her arm and leading her into the living room and closer to the other men.

"I don't appreciate being left out of conversations that have to do with my life. Now, I don't really give a rat's ass who you think you are, any of you." Dani eyed Vanderlan and then Van, Miele, Bently, Baher, and Randolph.

"I will not be ordered around or told that my destiny has been decided for me. Now get me my fucking clothes. I am so out of this loony bin."

She was about to walk away from them when Vanderlan uncrossed his arms and held her gaze with his own intense one. His eyes began to turn red, and at first she was fearful, but then came such a calming sensation she nearly lost her equilibrium.

"Come to me, Daniella," Vanderlan whispered. She wasn't certain if he'd said the words aloud or if she heard them in her head. She swallowed hard as the sensations enveloped her body. The voice could have been her pussy's voice, since that was the main body part that seemed to be at full attention right now. These men turned her into a horny, wanton woman.

She fought the sensation and shook her head. His eyes grew brighter red.

"Come to me now."

She began to walk toward him, and a feeling that it was only him and her filled her entire body.

She was inches from him, looking straight up, her head resting on her neck, her arms relaxed at her sides.

"You are not going anywhere, mate. You need protection, and your wolves and I will be providing that protection for you."

She shook her head.

"There will be punishments, mate, for disobeying us. Why don't you think about how pleasurable this will be for you? I guarantee, even your wolves will enjoy the sensations."

Dani felt all warm and tingly inside but then froze where she stood.

"No, Vanderlan. Stop it. You can't control me like this."

He appeared to be shocked that she stopped him, but if she allowed this, then she could be giving up her independence in their eyes.

"Dani, talk to me," he stated.

She took a deep breath and tried to organize her thoughts. She was annoyed at their ideas about controlling her and directing her so-called new life. She knew very little about them, yet now that she caused such a fuss, she realized that it didn't even matter. If what they said was true about mating for life, then they would have all the time in the world to get to know one another.

"Dani." Vanderlan raised his voice and she stared at him. "Tell me about yourself."

He raised his eyebrow at her in question, and she felt embarrassed a moment as she shyly clasped her hands in front of her.

"Tell me something about being a vampire."

He eased his hard expression and she saw his eyes sparkle just as a tingling sensation traveled over her skin.

Her nipples hardened to tight buds, her belly cramped and ached with need, and her pussy wept and felt so swollen.

"Please," she whispered, eyes closed and body swaying.

"I can tell you that vampires are superior beings. When we mate, it is for life. As you are learning, our blood mixes together and flows through one another."

"How?" she panted as she tried to maintain brain function while this superior vampire played her body like a musician strums their instrument.

"Magic, by the power of the gods, however, is not important, but the end result is what matters. You and I are one now. We are connected on the deepest levels and I assure you, our connection will only grow stronger. Now give me what I need, Dani. Supply your mate with pleasure. I want to taste what's mine, angel. Come closer to your master," he whispered, and she opened her eyes and locked gazes with him.

"Master?" she questioned him as the word rolled off her tongue. Why did calling this guy "master" turn her on?

She felt a hand on her waist. Then it trailed gently across her rib cage and on to her breast. It squeezed ever so tenderly.

"Oh," she moaned.

"That's right, sweet angel, feel what it is like to be touched by a vampire."

She felt another set of hands on her waist behind her, and then someone tugged her hair so she could turn toward him.

Van was there, his lips inches from her own.

He kissed her softly.

"Do you feel your desire for all of us, mate?" Vanderlan asked her, and she immediately nodded her head.

"Good girl, sweet Daniella. Van has something for you. Let him have all you have to offer."

She felt the fingertips graze over her T-shirt then to her boxers. A moment later she was divested of her clothing and standing there naked and fully aroused.

"Perfection." Vanderlan leaned down and licked across one of her nipples, the smoothness of his skin tickled her, and his scent aroused her. She had such an odd sensation inside of her. It was as if her blood pumped faster through her veins. He was familiar and she felt the need to reciprocate. She lifted her chin and tried to kiss him but he pulled back.

She felt herself sway until Van held her hips to steady her before he cupped her breasts. He lifted them higher causing both mounds to push out further toward Vanderlan's mouth.

She anticipated the feel of his lips or tongue, anything against her breasts. They hardened and tingled with need and she pushed out toward him. Vanderlan licked the tip of one breast then the other.

"Spread those thighs, sweet Daniella," Vanderlan demanded, and she did as she was told. She felt completely out of control yet utterly aware of every decision she made no matter how small. It seemed like her subconscious had more guts than her conscience.

Van's thick, calloused hands pressed down on her belly ever so slowly and straight to her pussy lips. She moaned and leaned her head back against his chest as Vanderlan lowered to his knees. His large hands expanded against her inner thighs, and she began to shake.

"So sweet." Vanderlan pressed one digit up into her pussy.

She moaned again and then rocked her hips against his finger.

"That's right, Daniella, your mates want all of you. Are you ready to have all of us?"

"Oh God, yes, please, I need," she begged of them and then held on to Vanderlan's shoulders as he added a second digit to her pussy.

In and out he pumped his fingers then leaned down lower to lick her flesh.

"Oh please!" she blurted out then began to thrust against his knuckles.

"That's it, sweet Daniella. So good. Doesn't it feel really good?"

"Yes, oh God, yes. More."

"Almost, Daniella. We're almost there." He teased her then plucked a nipple while he continued to thrust into her with his long, thick fingers.

She felt Van's hands cup and squeeze her breasts then go lower over her waist and straight to her mound.

"I smell your sweet cream, Daniella. I want to be inside of you," Van whispered against her neck then dragged his teeth across her delicate flesh. Something carnal came over her. She clenched her teeth and growled low.

"That's it, mate, embrace your true self. You are very special," Vanderlan whispered against her belly. He removed his fingers from her pussy and replaced them with his mouth.

"More!" she demanded, and he licked, sucked, and pulled on her clit. It was as if she was beyond her own body. The power within her was bubbling to the surface. She was hungry, needy, and she wanted so much it burned inside of her. She felt a burning again on the back of her neck and then Vanderlan's tongue and teeth against her inner groin.

Her pussy throbbed with need.

"I need you now, mate. I must be inside of you," Van stated, and she moaned and nodded her head.

"Please, Van, take me."

He needed no further push as she felt the tip of his cock against her well-lubricated pussy. He bent then pressed his cock into her faster than she expected but exactly how she needed.

"Yes!" she cheered him on and bent slightly forward as Van pumped into her pussy from behind. She felt wild, and salacious.

Vanderlan licked against her inner groin, making her moan.

"Your blood, my blood, calls to me, mate. I must taste you."

"I need so much!" she yelled as the tears stung her eyes, and she began to pant.

Van slowed his pace and kept one arm wrapped around her midsection snugly and his mouth against her shoulder and neck.

A moment later she felt the sharp pinch of pain against her inner groin as Vanderlan sucked at her skin. Her blood flowed through her. It practically echoed in her ears. Van pumped into her at full speed then bit into her neck and shoulder as she screamed her orgasm.

Her body jolted and thrust against Van's cock and Vanderlan's teeth and mouth as he sucked and took from her.

She couldn't breathe. She felt herself losing focus, and then she blacked out.

* * * *

"I can sense your anxiety, Van," Vanderlan whispered, being sure not to wake Daniella. She was calm, her breathing steady. He never thought that he would have a mate, never mind one so important and one he had to share with five Alpha wolves.

"My wolf does not like sharing a bed with a vampire," Van replied as he caressed Dani's long brown hair.

"Tell your wolf that it should get used to it. This is what is best for Daniella."

"I, personally, don't like these arrangements," Miele chimed in from across the room. Him, Bently, Baher, and Randolph were stretched out on the sofa and some recliners they'd brought in from the other rooms. They were insistent that they remain close by Daniella as well.

Vanderlan was impressed. He knew a lot about wolves and their mating rituals. But he never saw the exploration of finding a mate and claiming her this close before, and now it seemed she was meant to be his as well.

Daniella moaned as she turned her body to face Vanderlan. He caressed her cheek and softly rubbed his thumb over her bottom lip. She had lovely, full lips. He imagined those lips kissing his skin or wrapped around his cock while he caressed her long, silky brown locks.

She reached for him, touching his chest and snuggling closer. When she opened her eyes, she looked taken aback at first, and then she smiled. "It wasn't a hallucination?" she whispered.

"On the contrary, my love, it wasn't and is very real," he whispered, and she lowered her eyes, so sweetly and innocently. She was precious.

"Are you okay, Daniella?" Van asked, moving closer against her back as his arm wrapped around her midsection.

She looked up over her shoulder. Vanderlan could sense her emotions. She seemed fearful yet content. He hoped that she wouldn't regret what they shared or deny what was to come now that she had finally awoken.

"Are you angry with me?" she asked Van, surprising them both.

Van pressed his hand up her torso and under her chin and neck to turn her face toward him while Vanderlan caressed the palm of her hand, her wrist, and her lower arm. He could smell her arousal, and it grew stronger by the second.

"Never angry with you, Daniella, just wanting to protect you." He leaned down and kissed her softly on the lips. Vanderlan inhaled with his eyes closed. Her scent, that intriguing mix, was becoming stronger.

"It is my turn to claim you, mate," Vanderlan whispered then moved between her legs. She immediately opened to him and reached up to wrap her arms around his shoulders.

Vanderlan heard the low growls around him, and he looked to Van.

"It is time we claim her. All of us, so the bonding is sealed."

Van caressed Daniella's cheek, and she turned her face into his palm and kissed the skin.

"Are you sure, Daniella?" Van asked.

"I haven't a freaking clue, Van. The last forty-eight hours have been mind-boggling. Every part of me is saying this is right. I want all of you. It's crazy. I mean, I look at you, each of you and your exquisite bodies, good looks, and sexual appeal, and I become hungry for sex, for your touch, for anything you will give me. God, I can't believe I just said that out loud. I sound so desperate and needy, and I am not a needy, desperate woman."

Vanderlan smiled then caressed her cheeks. "It is perfectly normal, and we feel the same for you. Your scent, your enticing body, your need to fight your destiny turns us on and makes each of us want to claim you in every way possible. Tonight, we are going to make you all of ours, sweet Daniella." He shifted his body between her legs and slowly began to press his cock between her wet folds. "Easy, mate, I will be as gentle as you need."

Vanderlan lowered his body down over Daniella as he pushed the rest of the way into her.

* * * *

Daniella held on to Vanderlan. When she awoke between both him and Van, she was a bit nervous and wondered if the Fagan Pack would be angry with her for letting Vanderlan bite her. But she knew it was right and that it had to be done. There was this voice inside of her, a feeling deeper than gut instincts. It was something more and something she didn't recognize but since coming here had heard it more often. She sensed its need to be free and fight some sort of invisible barrier holding it back. She closed her eyes now and embraced the deep connection to Vanderlan. He was so sexy and good looking. She felt a silly, giddy feeling inside of her, like some schoolgirl virgin.

With every stroke of Vanderlan's cock, every caress of his tongue as he made love to her mouth, she felt a higher, more substantial power within herself. His lips had power, his hands were gentle yet solid, firm, possessive, and his cock was hard and thick. She felt every stroke stretch her vaginal walls, and as her body reacted and combusted, he moved faster into her. This was right. She needed to face the calling. She was a mate to five werewolves and a vampire. *Holy fucking shit!*

Over and over again Vanderlan stroked her pussy and made her body thirst for more. It was such an out-of-control feeling. It was as if she was beyond hungry and every stroke seemed to intensify the need within her instead of satisfying the need.

"I want, I need more." She gripped Vanderlan's shoulders and counterthrust up into him.

In and out he thrust into her then cupped her face between his hands and nibbled on her lips, her tongue, and her neck.

"So sweet. You are everything, Daniella."

He sat up, stretching her legs over his thighs just as Van reached for her hands and raised them above her head.

"Oh God, please!" she moaned as Van lowered toward her breast and took a taste. Her nipples hardened so taut and tight, and he teased her flesh. He pulled the pink protruding flesh between his teeth then licked and sucked the sting away.

She had two men touching her, caressing her, and giving her their full, undivided attention.

Vanderlan began to increase his speed as Van began to suck harder and tease her relentlessly. She felt her belly tighten, and then Vanderlan increased his speed and pumped his hips two more times. She moaned his name as he poured his seed into her then kissed her neck.

Van was rubbing and playing with her nipples still as Vanderlan caught his breath and caressed her cheeks.

"My sweet Daniella."

He slowly pulled from her body and began to leave the bed.

She watched his long, thick, fully aroused cock tap against his upper belly. He was a big man in all respects. He appeared as if he glided across the room instead of walked, and she wondered if his feet were even touching the floor. In her mind, she heard his voice.

"So much to learn and teach you, mate. The fact that you can hear me so quickly proves that you are mine."

"You can hear my thoughts?"

"I can, sweet angel."

"What about the others?" she asked, feeling a bit uncomfortable that her thoughts could be heard by Vanderlan and by the Fagan men. She was a bit insecure sometimes especially about her body.

"When the bond fully takes, they will be able to hear you as well. Your body is perfect, sweet Daniella. I intend on exploring it fully when there is more time."

She felt herself blush as she watched him. His body was filled with muscles upon muscles. His ass looked incredible as he walked toward the bathroom.

Then she felt the tips of Van's fingers against her chin.

"My turn." He leaned down to kiss her mouth. Daniella kissed him back with vigor and excitement. She wrapped her arms around his shoulders and squeezed him tight as he pressed between her thighs.

She felt the tip of his cock against her pussy, and she closed her eyes, tilted her head back, and accepted him.

"I feel so needy and I just had sex with a vampire and I want more," she whispered, and Van growled low against her neck, causing tiny tingling sensations to fill her to her belly.

"You are with me and my brothers now. I'll help to ease that hunger and satisfy you like no other."

"I heard that, wolf." Vanderlan's voice could be heard in the distance, and Van held Dani's gaze and he winked. It seemed that this was going to be a battle between wolves and a vampire, and she would be caught in the middle.

"But you shall reap the benefits," Vanderlan whispered in her mind then caressed her nipples somehow from a distance. She jerked and Van scowled.

"Enough, Vanderlan. She is ours now to make love to," Van stated firmly before lowering his mouth to hers and kissing her softly.

He took his time and she relished in the way he did it. The soft touch of his harder, manly lips against her skin ignited her desire. The way he rubbed his engorged cock back and forth, teasing her pussy, made her lift her hips to gain better contact. He knew what he was doing.

She tilted her lips upward to take a taste of him, and he teased her by pulling just out of her reach then nibbling on her chin and earlobe. She could feel the tip of his large cock against her wet folds. She was hungry again, in need of cock like an addict needed the drug of their addiction. She felt as if she could go insane without it.

"Please, Van."

He in return licked along her throat and straight to her lips.

"Mine," he stated firmly against her lips then pressed his cock forward, taking her completely in one fast thrust.

Van devoured her moans and began a series of slow, deep thrusts. She wrapped her legs tighter and caressed every part of his muscular body she could reach with her hands, and he continued to stroke her pussy with his cock. He would pull nearly all the way out, making her grasp for him and try to thrust up toward him so he would be fully inside of her, and then he shoved forward fast.

"Please, Van, please go faster," she begged of him. She needed every single one of those strokes.

He thrust again and again, trying to pick up speed but seeming as if he held back. Did he think that he would hurt her?

"Van, I feel so out of control and I would never be able to say this to a lover besides you, but I need so badly it burns inside. Please fuck me," she whispered.

She felt a bit embarrassed, but then she locked gazes with his glowing green and yellow eyes and something came over her.

She gripped his arms and tilted her pelvis upward. He in return pulled from her body, grabbed her around the waist, flipped her onto her belly, raised her thighs and ass up, then entered her from behind in one hard, fast stroke.

She screamed and then felt his hands on her hip bones, his fingers so thick and long they reached her groin and he stroked her with all he had.

"Mine." He growled. He actually growled and something inside of her responded. She growled back then pushed back against his cock.

Smack

She hadn't expected the slap to her ass, but the sting heightened her arousal. She wanted more so she thrust back again, growling low in the process.

Smack

She was utterly turned on by this, and then she felt the bed dip and then someone stroke her cheek. She glanced toward the side as Van continued to thrust into her pussy from behind, and there was Miele.

He held his cock in his hand, the tip revealed a drop of pre-cum and she licked her lips.

"That's right, mate, I want to feel that growling, hot mouth on my cock," Miele told her with his hazel eyes glowing partially yellow.

She opened wide, and he tilted his hips toward her. Just as she tasted the pre-cum on the tip and twirled her tongue over and around the mushroom top, Van smacked her ass and thrust into her hard.

She gasped as Miele took that moment to push his cock into her mouth.

"Oh fuck yeah, baby, that feels great," Miele told her, and she began to feast on him. His scent, musky and sweet, filled her nostrils. He placed one hand on her shoulder blade and the other under her so he could play with her needy breasts. His hips jerked against her, and she tilted her head back slightly to take more of him inside of her. She was filled with cock and every part of her tingled for more.

"That's it, baby, suck his cock good, and there's more where that came from," Bently stated. His voice aroused her just as Van thrust faster into her, rocking the bed, and nearly making her lose her rhythm sucking Miele's cock.

"Fuck, baby, I'm there." Van thrust over and over again, causing the bed to rock and creak before he poured himself into her. The next thing she felt was his mouth on her shoulder and his sharp teeth break her skin.

She screamed, releasing Miele's cock in the process as her body absorbed Van's essence. It was as if she felt it travel through her body. Before she could savor the sensations, Van was pulling from her, kissing her cheek and lips from behind her as his large hands caressed over her ass, squeezing and massaging her muscles.

"So fucking perfect." He wrapped his arm around her midsection and lifted her up.

She wasn't sure of his intentions until she saw Miele lying down with his legs hanging off of the bed.

His cock was fully enlarged as he held it in his hand and stared at her.

"I need you now, mate," he told her, and Van placed her on top of Miele.

Her pussy contracted, and she felt her cream drip down her thighs. She closed her eyes and moaned as she lifted up and Miele aligned his cock with her pussy. The moment she felt the tip of his mushroom top between her wet folds, she lowered herself, taking him fully inside of her.

His hands grabbed ahold of her hips and ass. His fingers stroked along the crevice of her ass cheeks then rubbed the round globes.

She began to thrust up and down on top of him. She felt empowered in this position and began a rhythm that satisfied her hunger for cock. She was lost in the pace, thrusting, and adjusting her pelvis so that with every stroke she felt his cock scrape harder against the inner muscles. She began to get more aroused, and then she felt the second set of hands on her back and ass.

"I love this ass, mate. This ass belongs to us."

Bently.

She moaned then opened her eyes as she slowed down and stared at Miele.

He moved his hand up over her hip, ribs, and breast then to her neck.

His fingers held her face, and his thumb caressed her lower lip. She continued to ride him while Bently massaged her ass cheeks and licked her spine.

"So fucking sexy," Bently whispered, and she stuck her tongue out to lick her dry lips and hit Bently's thumb. He moved it closer and she saw his eyes glow and his stare intensify. He liked that, so she did it again, but this time she pulled his thumb into her mouth and stroked it as if it was his cock.

A moment later she felt something cold and wet against her puckered hole. She gasped. Bently held her firmly. One hand on her face and chin the other against her thigh.

"Keep riding him, mate. We're going to fuck you together."

"Oh!" she moaned and the anticipation of having a cock in her ass aroused her beyond recognition. It was a fantasy to have more than one man fuck her, and tonight she was going to have that fantasy come true.

Bently gently pushed her shoulders down and Miele cupped her cheeks between his hands, pulling her toward him.

"I love your tits, baby. They're full and round and tasty."

He licked one nipple and pulled it between his teeth. She felt his cock grow larger inside of her pussy, and then she felt the tip of Bently's cock breach her puckered hole.

She inhaled and then Miele licked over her chin to her lips before plunging his tongue between them. He kissed her with passion and hunger. She kissed him back, and as he thrust his hips upward, she felt Bently push his cock through the tight rings.

It initially burned and felt odd, but then Miele stilled his cock within her pussy and Bently pressed fully inside of her ass.

"Fuck, you're so tight, so fucking hot." Bently growled.

"Oh God, please, it burns and I feel so full."

Bently pulled back then thrust into her. The lube he applied lubricated the unused muscles, and soon both men began to fuck her at once. Miele thrust upward then pulled down. Bently wrapped an arm around her waist so she was raised over Miele, and then he thrust in and out. She was never without a cock inside of her. They continued to make love to her, and she held on for the ride. Miele pulled her down lower as he thrust hard and fast upward. She felt his thigh muscles beneath her and knew he was strong and powerful to be able to continue such a rhythm in this position. Behind her, Bently held his cock halfway in her ass, giving Miele the room he needed.

She knew Miele was about to explode. She was nearly there, too, as she sucked along his neck then added teeth. That seemed to arouse him and send him over the edge.

"Fuck, baby, do that again. Bite me." Miele thrust rapidly upward. She did bite him a little harder, and it turned her on, she felt as if she could hear and almost taste his blood flowing through his veins.

"You can, Daniella. Bite him, taste from his blood and mark him." Vanderlan's voice echoed in her ears just as Miele exploded inside of her and bit into her shoulder. She wasn't sure what came over her, but she bit into Miele's shoulder and sucked from his blood. It tasted warm and metallic but sweet and fed the hunger growing inside of her. Miele growled and shook, and then Bently pounded into her ass as he growled like a wild beast.

His fingers felt like claws and his cock somehow felt longer, thicker and harder as he stroked her ass.

The orgasm overtook her, and Bently growled louder as he thrust hard then bit into her shoulder.

She screamed her release and rocked back against him.

"Fuck, baby, I heard him. I heard Vanderlan's voice and yours inside my head," Miele stated as he squeezed her to him. Bently was holding her, too, and crushing her with his heavy body.

"I can't breathe," she whispered, and both men chuckled as Bently pulled slowly from her ass. She wiped her mouth and was surprised that her teeth felt sharp.

"Hey." She pulled off of Miele.

"It's okay, Daniella," Vanderlan stated.

"I can't believe she bit him," Van stated.

"I can hear you talking with her. I felt her bite my brother and take from his blood," Baher stated, surprising them all. They looked around toward one another and nodded.

"You all heard Vanderlan and me and felt it, too? You felt what I felt?" Daniella asked. She was embarrassed and felt out of control for biting Miele, yet she was satisfied. Randolph and Baher were standing before her bare-chested and wearing only boxers.

She moved off the bed.

"It was fucking incredible," Randolph told her.

She lowered her eyes and felt her teeth move back to normal.

"Come here, baby." Randolph reached down and lifted her up into his arms. He held her against his chest and rubbed her back as he sat on the edge of the bed.

Tears filled her eyes.

She stared at him then looked around the room at the others. They seemed to be fine with all of this.

"I've lost my mind," she whispered, and Vanderlan scowled. She looked at him, and he held her gaze with a firm expression.

"You will not fight this. You belong to each of us. Let Randolph and Baher make love to you and mark you as theirs. The rest of us will be downstairs," Vanderlan stated.

"No. Don't go. I need you to stay."

Van and the others appeared upset. It wasn't that she just needed Vanderlan to stay. She needed them all here.

"I mean all of you must stay. I feel…incomplete unless you're all here. I don't understand it and I'm not the clingy type, God knows that, and so this is freaking ridiculous, but just forget it." She lowered her head.

Randolph kissed her neck.

"We all stay, then. Together we are one." Vanderlan walked over toward the bed and sat down next to her and Randolph.

Randolph eyed Vanderlan with concern.

"It's okay, Randolph," Daniella told him then cupped his cheeks and lifted up so he could remove his boxers.

He pulled them down, and then she kissed him, absorbing his scent and taste as she made love to his mouth.

He was so big and wide, she could hardly imagine wrapping her arms around him to hug him.

His hands caressed her back and ass and made her feel feminine and petite compared to him. She was concerned that she may hurt him again, and she tensed up a moment and released his lips.

"He will be fine now. You needed me here, Daniella, your blood contains mine and it was protected by me," Vanderlan told her.

What does that mean? My blood is protected by him. Like I need his protection? I can take care of myself. I have been for quite some time. Is this some macho vampire control thing? If so, he seems to have more in common with the Alpha weres than he thinks.

But his thoughts did ease her mind. It must have been some sort of vampire trick. She would have to Google it when she had a chance.

Vanderlan groaned as if her thought annoyed him, and she chuckled then looked into Randolph's eyes.

"Google?" he asked, and she widened her eyes in surprise. He had heard her thoughts, too. This could get sticky. She wondered how she could block them all from her thoughts.

Just then Randolph lifted her up, aligned his thick, long cock with her pussy and lowered her onto his shaft.

She closed her eyes and took him inside of her.

"You could never censor us from your thoughts, mate. We are all bound as one now," Vanderlan stated, and Randolph began to thrust up into her. She counterthrust in return.

They seemed awfully cocky, and it aroused her and made her want to fight them on it.

She grabbed Randolph's shoulders, thrust on top of him, then pushed him back to the bed so she was on top and in control.

Well, at least she thought she was until he pulled her down lower and covered her mouth in a salacious kiss while Baher prepared her ass to get fucked.

She was alive and wild with need. When she tried to thrust her hips, Randolph held her steady, with his cock hard and pulsating inside of her.

Then she felt Baher's hands on her hips, caressing her lower body and her ass. She was completely aroused when she felt the cool liquid as his finger pushed inside her ass.

She moaned against Randolph's mouth, his hold firm, and she was unable to move.

While he kissed her deeply, he ran his large hands over her arms and pulled them above his head. Her breasts stretched over his tight pectoral muscles, her ass lifted higher, and she felt Baher's cock push through the tight rings. In this position, bound with her hands above her, Randolph's very large cock hard inside her pussy and now another cock in her ass, she began to shake.

She was ready to orgasm and felt it tight within her womb.

Baher began to thrust into her, grabbing her hips and causing Randolph to pull his lips from her own. They gasped for air, but he continued to hold her hands. Her forearms remained leaning on his muscular chest. They began an in-and-out motion as she lifted higher, wanting to take them both fully inside of her. She was lost in emotion and the power within her when Baher thrust one last time, exploding inside of her ass as he bit into her shoulder from behind. She screamed a small release and rocked against Randolph's cock. She pressed back, and Randolph thrust upward, pulling her head and neck down against him.

He had released her hands and now she held on to him licking and sucking his neck as he thrust again and again. Baher pulled from her ass and Randolph rolled her to her back and began to stroke her cunt relentlessly. She was losing her breath with every stroke and panting for air. She wanted him so badly it hurt inside.

"Randolph." She moaned his name, and he lowered his face to her neck and licked and sucked the skin where his brothers marked her.

The bed rocked and creaked, and she grabbed his shoulders, ran her fingertips over his hair and neck, pulling him closer to her mouth. He continued to thrust into her with his hand cupped under her neck and head. It fit into his large, thick hands and aroused her even more.

"I feel it. Oh God, it's so strong," she admitted, and Randolph growled then pumped his hips and used his mouth and tongue to suck against her neck.

He bit into her shoulder as he poured himself into her, and she bit into his neck, feeding from him as she orgasmed hard, her body convulsing beneath his large frame.

They both panted and moaned. Then Randolph pulled slowly from her pussy and rolled to his side, taking her with him. She closed her eyes then cuddled close. The feel of his palm plastered across her ass were her final thoughts before sleep overtook her.

Chapter 10

Zespian stood in the meeting room. It was very late when the members of the Fennigan Pack arrived from Ireland. As members of the Secret Order, they were privy to information that even he wasn't. He got the call that they were arriving, and then he got the call from Van stating that Daniella was their mate and also the mate of the vampire Vanderlan. His heart pounded inside of his chest. He wondered what it all meant and hoped to get some answers. He had a feeling that his secret would be revealed. He wondered why the gods would make a vamp and five wolves the mate of one woman. Then Van had said they believed Daniella to be a healer. There were very few healers, and if she were the mate of wolves and a vampire then perhaps some bad things were headed their way. Over the past ten years, many rogues had targeted the Fagan Pack. They were a small pack, but they were just as intimidating and strong as some of the much larger ones. A relationship with Vanderlan had emerged over a century ago, and perhaps if that moment had not occurred, Zespian himself would have died soon after.

There was a knock at the door, and he knew it was them. The Fennigan Pack was here. The Fagan Pack would be getting some assistance in finding this killer.

He opened the door, and they each strolled in. They were some of the largest, meanest-looking men he had ever set eyes on. Their eyes were dark, they were dressed in black camo pants and black T-shirts. A contrast to their usual attire. Adrian was known to always be wearing an Irish kilt.

"Thanks for coming. I understand that you all have some insight into the case?" Zespian asked as he shook each of their hands.

"It appears ya got yourself a crazy doctor making hybrids, fucking with mother nature," Angus stated in a thick Irish brogue.

"Son of a bitch, I was afraid of this. Any clue who it is or where they're located?"

"Not so positive about the location, but our initial investigation leads us to the name Cartright," Adrian answered.

"What about the ones you have investigating the murders? Can we speak with them and go over the information found thus far?" Angus asked.

"Well, the Fagan Pack is now working the case. The detective who was taking over is their mate. They found out when I called them in to try to catch the rogue wolf. Now what you're telling me makes more sense. This thing was created in a lab?"

"It seems to be. So the Fagan Pack found their mate. That's fucking great. She a good-looking woman?" Brady asked with a chuckle.

Zespian smiled. These men were always teasing one another. It should be fun to have the Fagan Pack and the Fennigan Pack together again.

"She's a bit of an independent woman with a lot of attitude. Apparently not too keen on being told what to do. They're working on her acceptance as we speak. I'd like to show you what we have so far in the case and the leads we were after. Then you can visit with the Fagan Pack and Dani, their mate and the detective working the case."

"Her name is Dani?" Delaney asked.

"Short for Daniella," Zespian added.

"Very nice. It should be fun to visit them," Adrian added with a chuckle. Then they all sat down to go over the material they had thus far.

Chapter 11

The horrific sounds echoed in the large arena. A test of sorts to confirm the control of the enforcer was being administered. Marfur Cartright looked on in both awe and disgust. This creature appeared as a strikingly handsome man, large and powerful, and when it transitioned into its wolf, it became unstoppable.

He heard the numerous screams from the men set forth to challenge the beast. It appeared that when the enforcer was in wolf form, it followed orders to the fullest when issued a kill order. Marfur really didn't see that as a problem. He just worried that the beast might cause a major mess in the process.

"I have a concern. This hybrid is supposed to mix with wolves and humans while accomplishing his mission. He will need to adapt to every environment while hunting. How can you ensure me and my leader that this will not blow up in our faces?"

"He knows what to do. Plus, if he was to go overboard in a killing spree, we made it so that Detrix will take the fall. While the investigative team hunts for Detrix, the enforcer will be taking out numerous leaders of the Fagan Pack, minimizing their ability to fight back," Porter stated.

"I thought the plan was to lure in Detrix with the victim that escaped so we could kill him off?" Marfur asked.

"We thought about it, and decided that perhaps Detrix could be useful after all. It seems that Dr. Evans had made some adjustments in Detrix's thinking when he was created. Detrix, in his journey to destroy the Fagan Pack, also needed to keep an eye out for any powerful beings that your commander Dismar could use. For example, a fairy with magic powers, a healer, which is quite rare, or any other magical being that may help to strengthen the Cartright Pack and help to maintain Dismar's position in the circle while overtaking Fagan territory."

"So you believe that Detrix may have found such a creature?" Marfur asked, feeling the excitement for such a discovery.

"It is quite possible," Dr. Evans stated.

"But how can he be trusted to bring his discovery here? He escaped your control already."

"He may have decided to venture off on his own because of the tainted vampire blood, but ultimately he is to serve me. He will return and perhaps with a special package in hand," Dr. Evans stated with a smile, and Marfur nodded his head.

"Interesting. I look forward to seeing what happens."

* * * *

Dani finished taking a shower and drying her hair. Margo had brought over some clothes for her to wear, so Dani began to get dressed.

She was standing in front of the mirror wearing only her black dress pants and black bra. She was about to pull on her burgundy dress shirt when she sensed someone standing near the doorway.

"What do you think you're doing?" Randolph asked her.

Dani pulled the shirt on and turned toward him as she began to button the dress shirt.

"What does it look like I'm doing?" She had been very careful not to project her thoughts to any of the men since this morning. It had been tricky trying to not think at all while planning to go back to work.

"It appears as if you may be thinking of leaving the estate."

She felt her fingers shaking, and she released her hold on her shirt and placed her hands on her hips. She wasn't wearing any shoes, so

Randolph towered over her. Not that shoes would matter anyway, the man was definitely taller than her. They all were, including Vanderlan.

"Am I a prisoner?" she asked him.

He stared at her. It was a hard stare and she felt like he was trying to read her mind or speak telepathically to her. She held her ground until Vanderlan's voice and Van's voice chimed in, too.

"You are not leaving the estate."

"Damn you!" she blurted out loud then covered her ears with her hands. "I am not listening to you. I have a job to do and finding this killer is my job."

"Not anymore," Randolph stated firmly as he unfolded his arms and walked toward her.

He reached out and helped to rebutton her blouse. As she looked down, she realized that she had screwed up the order of buttons. Obviously, Randolph knew he intimidated her.

She inhaled, catching his scent and immediately feeling the urge to cuddle.

"You want to cuddle?" he teased her.

"Fuck!" she blurted out in frustration and tried to take a retreating step away from his hands. He was making her lose focus.

"That sounds even better," he teased, and she shook her head.

"You're confusing me."

"I haven't said much."

She stared at him. To think of it, Randolph spoke more to her than ever before. She was so frustrated and he knew it.

"Take my hand. We need to go over a few things downstairs."

"And if I refuse, will you lock me in a bedroom?"

"Chain you to the bed naked and spread out for our enjoyment would be more appealing," Bently chimed in.

She shook her head. Bently was a tease and a flirt.

She began to walk past Randolph and toward the chair that contained her gun, badge, and other belongings.

"You won't need the gun."

"I may need it to get out of this house."

"Not unless there are silver bullets in it."

"Whatever," she stated then walked out of the room empty-handed.

* * * *

Dani entered the living room to find all the men standing and sitting around, waiting for her and Randolph to arrive.

She paused a moment as the sight of them, all together in a room, took her breath away. They were so beautiful. They looked so amazing individually and lethal standing before her all together. She placed her hand over her quivering belly and took a few unsteady breaths. The back of her neck tickled. As Randolph placed his hands on her shoulders and pressed his chest against her back for support, she released another sigh.

She'd had sex with five wolfmen and a vampire. A series of insecure thoughts entered her mind. She lost control of her ability to block any of her thoughts. She clutched her stomach and took a step away from Randolph.

These were Alpha males, good-looking men who were centuries old and could have their choice of any woman they ever wanted. Plus, she didn't do commitments. She was bad at relationships. Look what happened between her and her booty-call buddy?

A series of growls went through the room, shocking her back to the present. In a matter of seconds, Vanderlan was in front of her. She attempted to take a step back.

"I think we should slow this down a bit."

A moment later she was practically plastered against his solid chest, his arms wrapped tight around her waist while his other hand cupped her neck and head. He gave her hair a little yank.

"Booty-call buddy?" he questioned her.

"Dani?" Van asked as he stood to the side of Vanderlan.

She panicked a moment. They were jealous? Could she handle that?

"Stop this. Stop reading my thoughts. Get out of my head. I need some breathing room. I feel like I'm on a roller coaster that has no breaks." She rambled on until she sensed the tingling sensation travel through her body. She closed her eyes and began to relax in Vanderlan's arms. Van caressed her shoulders as he pressed his body against her back. She was sandwiched between him and Vanderlan. She calmed her breathing and absorbed how damn good it felt being this close to them, touched by them and cared for by them.

She absorbed Van's thumb as it rubbed gently back and forth over the back of her neck. With every swipe, she felt a tug inside, like an imaginary rope that led from their touch straight to her pussy.

Vanderlan kissed her softly on the lips. She moaned and swayed. Van continued to gently rub the one spot behind her neck and below the hairline. Vanderlan released her lips and continued to kiss along her neck and shoulder.

"What are you doing to me?"

"Loving our woman," Van replied.

"Taking care of you, Daniella," Vanderlan whispered against her skin.

"It feels so good. What's back there on my neck? It's like an imaginary rope that's connected from where you're touching me, straight to my—" She didn't say the word. She couldn't say the word and instead she thought it. *Pussy.*

"You belong to us, Daniella. The gods have spoken. You are so very special in many ways. We will teach you and show you what more you are capable of. That sensation you feel comes from our connection. We share a bond stronger than most. There is a star tattoo on the back of your neck. It is our eternal connection to you and you to us," Vanderlan told her.

"You feel it every time we are close and you want to pull away from us. It burns and you rub at it trying to ease that need. But you can't, Daniella. It represents our union. All of us," Van explained.

Dani reached up to touch the spot, and her fingers crossed Vanderlan's as Van guided her to the exact spot. While all three of them touched it, she felt the intense warm sensation filter through her. A moment later, Miele, Randolph, Bently, and Baher touched her, too, and she totally relaxed and embraced their possession of her.

"That's it, mate. We are all one. We will protect you, guide you, and watch over you always." Bently kissed her softly on the lips.

One by one they released her, and Van took her hand and led her toward the couch in the living room.

* * * *

"So there are some things we need to discuss. The Fennigan Pack will be joining us on the hunt for the rogue wolf," Baher stated. His need to keep Dani nearby at all times was consuming his thoughts. It had been difficult to think of a plan with his brothers and Vanderlan to find the rogue and to keep Dani safe. He had a feeling that she wouldn't stay put no matter what they told her or how much they seduced her.

"Rogue wolf? What does that mean?" Dani asked.

"It means a wolf who no longer follows pack rules and has gone out on their own. Sometimes they have the assistance of other rogues whose ultimate goal is to overrule a pack or the rules of the circle of elders. It can be for many reasons."

"So this wolf, Baher, is rogue? Do you think there are others?" Dani asked.

"I hope that there aren't, but we can't be certain. This particular wolf is causing quite the mess and needs to be stopped," Bently replied.

"Through our sources, we found that he has been lying low since the attack in the apartment a few days ago. We fear that he is looking for you, Dani. He is wolf enough to sense that you are unique. You're a healer, Dani, and that means you are very valuable to our race," Miele answered.

"Because you have been chosen as the mate to our pack, the Fagan Pack, and also to Vanderlan, we believe that it is for good reason. Our pack has been under attack by rogue wolves on and off for centuries. We are one of the smaller packs in the world with only fifty thousand pack members," Van stated.

"Fifty thousand seems like a lot of wolves. What does the largest pack contain?" Dani asked.

"Many packs have members in the hundreds of thousands," Bently told her.

"The point is that we are a strong and solid pack. The location of our land and pack territory is crucial to maintaining a position and representation in the pack order. We have ties to many other packs and affiliated groups that maintain justice and survival for our race. The fear of possibly being taken over has grown over the past ten years. Someone out there wants our territory. They have gone to great lengths to destroy us. We've lost many members to murder or crimes that really didn't look like actual crimes, but looked like setups," Baher explained.

"So you think someone is after your territory? Margo explained to me about the circle of elders and how they are the ultimate power over the packs and maintaining peace. Can't they step in?" she asked, and Van smiled.

"They can only do so much. They are kept busy day in and day out with maintaining protocol and handling pack law. It is kind of like survival of the fittest and we are being challenged."

"Well, if I have these powers or whatever they are to help, then perhaps this might strengthen your fight."

"Right now only a few know of your existence. We think it is in your best interest to speak with Margo and train with her. She is a healer and can help you to learn about your abilities and what your position means."

Dani crossed her arms in front of her chest and gave him the evil eye. "And while I'm safe and secure in some bedroom with another healer, the rest of you get to go out and hunt down this rogue wolf? I don't think so."

"Daniella, this is not up for discussion," Baher stated. He was truly getting annoyed with her attitude and recalcitrant behavior.

She stood up and placed her hands on her hips. "Not up for discussion? Bullshit! I am not some weak female who is going to bow down to any of you and sit inside some security room and act all girly while the rest of you risk your lives hunting this asshole. I'm in and involved in the investigation, or I'm not speaking with Margo and learning about this healing stuff."

Baher stepped forward and grabbed her around the waist, hoisting her up against him.

They were both breathing heavy, and their hearts were racing.

"You have got to be the most stubborn woman I have ever met in my entire life," Baher told her through grinding teeth.

"Well, then you haven't been to the right places or lived in the real world. Most women are not damsels in distress, mister. They are independent, well-trained, and get-the-job-done professionals. Get used to it, or we're going to be fighting every minute of every day."

He shook his head at her in frustration then turned her around to face the others as he wrapped his arms around her midsection.

"So what are we going to do with her?" Baher asked his brothers, and everyone stared at Dani.

* * * *

Dani was feeling crazy. Every time one of the men made a comment like this one Baher just made, she felt such a sexual pull and need that she completely forgot why she was arguing with them to begin with. Randolph gave her a knowing smirk, and it both made her annoyed and made her smile.

"You know this isn't fair, don't you? I've been in law enforcement since I entered the police academy when I was twenty years old. This is what I do. Investigation is my life, and I don't think I should have to give that up."

They were all silent a moment.

"There will be no need for you to do it anymore," Vanderlan stated in a deep voice.

When he spoke, she felt it in every part of her. There was a different connection than with the Fagan brothers. The intensity was the same, but with Vanderlan she felt it in her veins. It must have something to do with the whole blood and vampire thing.

"It is more than that, Daniella. You have no idea how difficult this is for us to be sharing you. As a vampire, I do not share. I have done my part in providing assistance to many types of mythical creatures and shifters, but, just like the wolves, I have searched all my life, centuries, for a mate, and here you are, and it seems that I must share you with wolves. It does not sit well with me. Just as I am certain it does not sit well with the Fagan Pack. But we all know that there is a higher power than our own desires and hang-ups. As my mate, I will do whatever I need to do to protect you and keep you by my side. You going off on a hunt for a beast that has gotten your scent and now craves you is not an option I am willing to even consider."

"But, Vanderlan, I, too, am struggling with this entire concept. As a human, being sexually involved with more than one man at one time is slutty and taboo. Yet you all expect me to just accept it. You also expect me to give up everything I have worked hard for and achieved, yet you all give up nothing. How is that fair?"

"You will be quite busy as the Alpha female to the Fagan Pack. There will be many responsibilities for you, just as I am certain Vanderlan will have some for you as well," Van replied.

She crossed her arms in front of her chest as Baher released her.

"I am not ready to give up my life and my career. I want it both, and I would appreciate it if you all could take the time to try to work this out. I can help you. Let me remain involved with the investigation." A collective sigh went through the room. She could hear their thoughts. They wanted to keep her under wraps. They wanted to make love to her, hold her in their arms, and keep her safe. She saw their fear of this rogue trying to capture her, kill her, or take from her what it wanted. She felt it all as she closed her eyes and tried to remain strong.

"Please give this a try, and I promise to try my hardest to understand and submit to your demands as wolves and as a vampire. God that sounds so crazy," she stated, and then Baher turned her around and pulled her into his arms.

"You are stubborn, woman." He kissed her softly on the lips. She fell right into his trap as he made love to her mouth, while his hands explored her body and caressed her from ass to shoulders then back over her ass again.

As he released her lips, she hugged him back.

"One more thing," she stated, and they sighed in annoyance.

"Do I really need silver bullets to kill a wolf?" she asked.

"You won't need anything because you won't be getting close enough," Baher replied.

"There's something else you all are going to have to learn about me. I like guns. I like all types of guns and I enjoy going to the range and letting off some steam. I'm a homicide detective and I have a license. I want my guns. I want to carry my weapon and I want to be prepared. It is who I am and you all need to accept that."

They thought it over but without her hearing their words. They blocked her.

"I will get them for you. You can load your Glock and be prepared as you ask." Randolph rose from the chair and exited the room.

The doorbell rang and Bently walked out of the living room to answer the door.

"That should be Margo. Can you be a good mate and accept her help in showing you what it means to be a healer?" Vanderlan asked in an annoyed tone. She was a bit taken aback by it but realized that was his vampire arrogance showing through. He was a superior creature and man. She knew that he had the ability to destroy most anything in his path and a bit of trepidation reached her heart. A moment later she felt the cool hand touch her shoulder. He had been directly in front of her, leaning against the couch, and now he was behind her, moving her hair away from her neck and whispering against her skin.

"Do not fear me, mate. I adore you already and would never do you harm." He kissed her skin. His warm breath traveled through her body. "Besides, you are way too tasty." He licked her skin then gently ran his sharp teeth across her neck and firmly against the vein. She shook with anticipation, feeling her own need to be bitten by him fill her to her soul. "Later," he told her as Margo and Bently entered the room.

Chapter 12

"Okay, so let me get this straight. You're telling me that as a healer, I have magical powers within me to heal even those who may be dying?"

"Well, technically yes. However, you cannot use it freely. Normally a healer is temporarily selected to provide this service to mythical creatures or whomever the gods feel it necessary to maintain power and justice. We, as healers, are never betrothed to anyone. We are free spirits when not serving. This is what makes your situation so outrageous and wild. To be betrothed, destined to be the mate of the wolf pack you are sent to help protect is rare. I'm not saying it has never happened, but it is rare. But then add in the vampire, too, and holy shit, the entire concept is insane," Margo stated.

"That's wonderful. So, I'm the first this has ever happened to. Is that bad?" Dani asked, feeling instant anxiety until Vanderlan sensed her worry and intervened. He began to console her and calm her worry. He was always there for her, and it both freaked her out and comforted her. She felt the others as well and Van projected some anxiety about the visit from the Fennigan Pack.

"Not bad per se but actually pretty damn amazing. It can only lead me to believe that you are destined to provide much-needed help along the way. Your wolves and the vampire will need your healing powers as they fight to maintain their standing and control of Fagan Pack territory. I cannot foresee what is to come, but if the gods have sent you here and have hidden you like this for this long, then there is something brewing."

"Like what? Do you think there are more rogues out there?" Dani asked, feeling instant concern for her men.

"It is probable. So I think we should begin to explore your powers. There is really nothing to it as long as your heart is pure and remains focused for the right reasons. It is one of the fool-proof ways to ensure that a healer doesn't stray from good to bad. You can't heal an evil spirit. The gods have the ultimate power.

"So if a rogue or whomever tries to capture or exploit a healer, then they will not succeed. Unfortunately it leaves you with little power to defend yourself. However, you are different in that way, too. You are a fighter. You have your obsession with weapons and upholding the law. I am not certain of what is to come, but this current battle may only be the beginning."

"Well, I guess we should get as prepared as possible. Although I think you may be wrong about the level of my involvement in this. The men seem to want to keep me out of this. I won't be able to do that. I want to catch this rogue wolf. He has killed so many innocent people. While you explain things to me, can you also show me how to block my thoughts from them fully. They're making me crazy by answering my thoughts and listening in then talking at the same time. It's freaky. Besides, there are some things I would really like them to not know about."

"Ohh, like what?" Margo teased.

"Well, earlier I panicked when I entered the room and saw them there. It was overwhelming to me to see them like that after we had sex. They are so very handsome and, well, appealing to every part of me. It was scary and I panicked about our relationship. I don't do commitment, Margo. You know that."

"You mean like your relationship with the cop, Jack?"

Dani blushed. "You knew about him?"

"Honey, he was a fine-looking man and a great body in that uniform of his."

Dani chuckled as she thought about Jack.

Then she felt a pinch to her ass cheek and jumped.

"Ouch!"

"Watch it!" all six men stated firmly, and she swallowed hard.

"They heard you?" Margo asked, looking as if she felt guilty and to blame.

She took Dani's hand as Dani rubbed her sore ass cheek.

"We'll work on that first before we go any further. Your mates don't need to know all the details around your abilities anyway."

"Won't they get mad at us?" Dani asked.

Margo smiled as they took a seat on the long sofa.

"No worries, us women have to stick together."

* * * *

Miele was making lunch, and Van and Vanderlan were getting updates on some information as they waited for the Fennigan Pack to arrive.

Dani was talking with Bently and Baher in the study when Randolph arrived. He closed the door behind him, and she immediately saw her Glock in his hands.

She locked gazes with him as he approached.

"It's all set with silver bullets." Randolph handed over the Glock, handle forward.

She reached for it and he held on to it.

"This is serious stuff. It will kill most anything and it kills wolves."

She swallowed hard. She felt the intensity in the room. She knew this was very difficult for them and that they truly trusted her to hand this over to her. The silver was their weakness.

"You handled it okay, Randolph?" Bently asked with concern. He projected his reasoning behind his question to Dani as Randolph released the gun to her.

Just touching it could have seriously injured Randolph. He'd used some sort of special gloves to handle it.

"I wanted her to be safe," Randolph stated.

Dani swallowed. Then she turned to point her gun up toward the window as if practicing to aim it like she missed holding it in her hands. Truth was that she did. She liked guns and having them. She just didn't like to shoot people with them. Knowing that she had this power of the silver bullets humbled her obsession. But as she thought about the rogue wolf and its potential to do her men harm, she felt confident.

She lowered the weapon, and Randolph was instantly there to take it from her hands. She wasn't certain why until he passed the Glock to Bently who placed it in a drawer by the bookshelf.

Randolph pulled Dani into his arms and cupped her neck and head before leaning down to kiss her fully on the mouth.

In an instant, that kiss turned hotter. He lifted her up, and she straddled his waist as he devoured her moans.

She was against the wall a moment later as Randolph began to unbutton her blouse and divest her of her bra and the top she wore.

She helped him as they released lips to undress. Her breasts bounced as he pulled off his shirt, revealing muscles and tattoos galore.

"Fuck, Dani, you holding a gun turns me on." He ravaged her mouth again. They were both on a mission to conquer that kiss, and soon he was lowering her feet to the floor to remove the rest of her clothing.

She tore at Randolph's pants, helping him so they were both naked and skin to skin. As their bare bodies touched, they both moaned.

He lifted her up again so that she could straddle him as he walked over to the couch.

Her pussy dripped with cream, the anticipation of having his long, thick shaft inside of her, fucking her, made her hungry.

He fell to the couch, and she adjusted her legs as she squatted above him.

He pulled her head and neck down so Randolph could kiss her. His tongue plunged into her mouth, and her breathing grew rapid as they both moaned with need.

She felt the tip of his cock at her pussy lips as she lifted up so she could take him in. He released her hair and neck, grabbed her hips, and pushed down while he thrust his hips upward.

"Oh!" she screamed as his hard cock invaded her needy pussy. Up and down he thrust his cock into her, causing her to lose any bit of ability to assist. Instead, she relished in the pleasure he was bringing her.

She felt the hands on her shoulders. Then Randolph slowed his thrusts down.

A kiss to her neck, a nibble on her earlobe. She rolled her head back against Bently's chest. His hard cock tapped against her lower spine and she moaned.

"I've got something for you, mate. You're so beautiful," he said. Then she felt the cool liquid press into her anus. She jerked, and Randolph thrust up again and again.

A moment later she felt the tip of his cock at her back entrance then him slowly push into her.

She lowered her cheek against Randolph's shoulder and neck and began to lick, nibble, and suck his skin.

"Fuck, Dani, I can't take that," Randolph told her then both men began to thrust into her one after the other. She was fully aroused ready to burst when Randolph beat her to it. He held her so tight as he thrust repeatedly up into her pussy. His large hand cupped her neck and face, and he growled his release, exploding inside of her. She held her breath then released it as she pushed back against Bently's cock.

"Fucking beautiful." Bently began a series of long, hard strokes into her ass. He reached down and spread her ass cheeks wider while he pumped his hips over and over again.

Randolph pulled her to him as he licked along her shoulder where the bite marks had been inflicted but healed instantly because of her gift.

For a moment she wished they had remained so she could show them what they meant to her and that she accepted their claiming.

Bently continued to fuck her in the ass then grabbed a fistful of hair while he leaned down and sucked at the tattoo on her neck. She felt it burn, and then he exploded inside of her, pumping three more times before lying against her as he caught his breath.

He slowly pulled from her body and kissed her shoulders.

"Ours forever," he stated, and Randolph repeated the sentiment.

He slowly lifted her up off of him and into Baher's arms.

Before she could recover from her first round of lovemaking, Baher had her spread out on the large round table with her legs wide open and his palms holding her in place as he licked along her pussy lips. He ate at her cream and was relentless with his tongue and teeth.

She rolled her head side to side and then felt his tongue thicken and elongate. He told her what he was doing.

"One of the many benefits of being with a wolf, mate."

Dani couldn't give a verbal response. She was moaning and gyrating her pussy against his tongue on the verge of exploding when he stopped and pulled his wolf tongue from her pussy.

"No, please do that again," she begged of him.

"You are too mouthy of a mate. I think you need to learn some control of that tongue."

"What? Come on Baher. It feels so good."

"Who is the Alpha male here?" he teased her then licked across her nipple and bit gently as he pulled her ass closer to the edge of the table.

She bent her knees as she squealed.

"You are my woman and I decide what is best for you."

He lined his cock up with her pussy and pressed into her hard. She reached for his shoulders and held on to him as he thrust again and again into her. She felt the hard wood against her ass, and as he pressed deeper and harder with every stroke, she felt her ass cheeks spread and her oversensitive puckered hole hit the surface.

"Oh!" she screamed, and Baher continued to stoke her pussy as he licked and sucked her nipples.

"I'm going to come!" she yelled at him, and he stopped. She wondered what was happening. She wondered why he would do that.

He held her gaze with his own. His hazel eyes showed specks of yellow. His wavy brown hair looked messy and oh so sexy.

"You come when I say," he told her.

Oh God, he's so sexy and demanding.

Baher thrust his cock into her once then pulled nearly all the way out. Her body jerked with the motion.

He pressed her arms up above her head as he towered over her. What a sight she must be, spread open wide and naked on top of a table in the study.

"I like you like this. All spread out before me to feast on with your hands held above your head. One day real soon I'm going to tie you up to the bed, spread eagle so I can lick, suck, bite, and fuck you."

"Oh God!" She moaned as a flow of cream dripped from her pussy.

"I think she might like that, Baher. Good call," Bently teased and Randolph chuckled.

Baher thrust his cock into her again. This time, two strokes.

"More. Please let me come." Her belly tightened, her pussy ached, and she wanted to come. Just a few more strokes of his hard, thick cock and she was there.

She tried to push toward him and his hold on her arms tightened as he used his hips to hold her in place.

"I'm in charge, remember."

"Please, Baher, I need you."

"Tell us you like to be controlled. Tell us how turned on you are right now being restrained while I fuck you." Baher tormented her, and it turned her on.

"Fuck yes. I love it! I want more. Give it to me!" she yelled, and he chuckled then smiled.

"As you wish, mate."

She nearly lost focus as Baher thrust his cock into her pussy at record speed. The table creaked and moaned from his thrusts, and she held tight, waiting for him to allow her to come. Holy shit was she completely turned on by this.

"Let me come, let me come, let me come," she begged.

"Almost, just a little longer."

"Now please now."

"Just a little bit longer..."

He thrust his hips and released her hands to grab her hips and hold on tight while he went deeper and harder.

"Now!" he yelled as he exploded inside of her, and she followed, screaming his name and panting for air.

"Holy fuck, Dani. That was amazing." Baher pulled slowly from her pussy then pulled her up into his arms. They hugged each other and both tried to catch their breath.

He cupped her face between his hands.

"I love you, mate. You complete me." Baher kissed her before she could respond.

Chapter 13

Randolph held Dani's hand as they walked from the bedroom to the kitchen downstairs. She could hear the roars of laughter and some pretty relentless teasing going on. The only one who seemed a bit distant was Vanderlan.

As she arrived at the kitchen, all laughter stopped, and she froze in place.

Holy shit!

Six very large, tattooed men stared directly at her and eyed her like the last piece of candy in a candy jar. She felt exposed as they sniffed the air.

"This is Dani," Van stated as he introduced her.

"I'm Adrian and no offense, love, but you're too fucking hot to be called a boy's name." He kissed her hand and bowed before her. She smiled as she said hello, getting the impression that Adrian was a flirt and a half.

"I'm Brady and this is Delaney and Eagen," Brady stated then shook her hand and bowed as he kissed it. Their Irish brogues were charming. Delaney followed suit, kissing her hand and eyeing her over as he sniffled a little closer to her.

"Watch it." Randolph stated firmly, and the men chuckled. She wasn't sure if Randolph was teasing or not.

"I'm Quinn, the handsomest and most charming of the Fennigan Pack," Quinn stated then kissed her hand and winked at her. Perhaps he was the flirt of the family?

"This is Angus, he is lead Alpha of the group of troublemakers." Van introduced the leader, and he nodded his head and shook her hand.

"It's nice to meet you all," she responded then stepped back, placing her hand on her hips as she rested her palm on the holder where her gun sat.

"A fucking cop. Holy shit. And a detective, no less. You fuckers are up shit's creek ya know?" Adrian teased.

"She finds out about some of your illegal activities and who knows what she'll do," Brady added.

"It might be kind of fun having the lassie handcuff one of them or all of them and having her way with them," Delaney added, and they all laughed.

"With that body and her weapons, she might just be the Alpha of the group," Eagan teased, and they began to carry on like a bunch of schoolboys. The Fagan Pack joined in ribbing the men on their lack of women and whatever.

Randolph held her by her waist, and she laughed as the friendly teasing continued.

"We need to discuss our plan for tonight," Vanderlan stated firmly, and all conversation and laughter stopped.

Vanderlan held her gaze, and she sensed his feelings of displacement. She in return consoled him, and he crunched his eyebrows at her then blocked her attempts.

What the fuck was that about? I was just trying to help.

"We need to make a plan. Who will be going where to check out which locations?" Vanderlan asked.

"Fennigan Pack can split up and check those two bars and the hotel where our sources believe a rogue fitting the same description as the one we're looking for has been frequenting," Bently stated.

"There was another place that he was spotted weeks ago. A few of us could go there," Adrian suggested.

"Wait, before Baily was killed, she had mentioned seeing this rogue at the café she and her sister hung out at. There's also a club right on the same block. Her sister was one of his victims," Dani stated.

"Really? Well, what's the name of the place? We can check it out," Angus said.

"It's called Fantasia. It's located on Chester Street," Dani replied. Quinn pulled out a small device and began typing. A few minutes later he explained what he found.

"It's a night club, owned and operated by Cysure Corp."

"Cysure Corp? Why does that name sound familiar?" Van asked aloud.

"Fuck!" Vanderlan yelled then slammed his fist down on the island.

"What is it?" Van asked.

"I should have realized this sooner. With finding Dani and everything else that has been happening, I completely lost focus."

"Thanks a lot," Dani replied sarcastically and gave him a dirty look before turning away. That was for his response to her comforting him earlier.

"Over a year ago, while I was away in Ireland, assisting the Fennigan Pack, someone broke into my estate down south. I simply thought it was hired help, a young man desperate for the finer things in life. Anyway, some items were taken, and I sensed that my vault where vials of blood are stored was tampered with. But my personal, more valuable supplies are well hidden under magic besides locks and other things. I keep decoys more accessible and they are tainted with magic," Vanderlan explained.

"So what does that have to do with Cysure Corp?" Van asked.

"Cysure Corp is involved with numerous types of businesses, including medical technology. They are an international company. I'm not certain who exactly the owner is, but they have a lot of money and a lot of connections."

"I'm still not understanding you," Van pushed.

"This is just a guess, but what if it wasn't the kid that stole from me, but perhaps someone connected to Cysure Corp that needed the blood of a strong vampire to use in experimentation?"

"Holy shit, this rogue wolf seeks the blood of its victims. Every crime scene is a major mess," Dani stated, and they all looked at her.

"You said the blood was tainted, Vanderlan. With what?" Dani asked.

"A curse, really. The rogue wolf would become so desperate for a certain blood that it would eventually go insane and take its own life."

"But does this blood contain your real blood?" she asked.

"Sure, it has some of it, or I wouldn't be able to taint it."

"What are you thinking, Dani?" Bently asked her.

"If there is enough blood of Vanderlan's running through this rogue wolf's bloodstream, then won't it also sense the things that Vanderlan desires? I mean his attraction to me? His ability to identify my special abilities," she stated, unsure that the Fennigan Pack knew she was a healer.

"Oh shit!" Van stated.

"This is really strange." Quinn continued to type away on the device.

"Stand in my shoes the last seventy-two hours and you'll see strange," Dani stated sarcastically, and Vanderlan aimed a very deep, dark stare at her. He was trying to command her or something, but she blocked him just as he had done to her and just as Margo had taught her.

"This club Fantasia owned by this company has a big event going on tonight. I say we go there, investigate it, and see if we can track down the owner. Maybe identifying the owner of Cysure Corp will help us figure out who's responsible for creating the rogue," Quinn suggested.

"That sounds perfect. Randolph, do you have an ankle holster I can borrow so I can hide my gun under my pants?" Dani asked, and silence filled the room.

"You are not going anywhere," Van stated firmly.

"I think that is our clue to leave," Angus stated, and his brothers chuckled.

"We'll set everything up and meet you guys out front in an hour," Angus stated, and the men left the room.

* * * *

"You can't be serious? I know where that location is. I know the clubs around there," Dani stated with her hands on her hips.

"Did you not hear what Vanderlan said? This rogue could have his blood running through his veins. You are a healer and you are our mate. Tonight and from here on out, you are no longer a detective working the case," Van said.

She was shocked, and she was not going to stand there and take this.

"What a load of chauvinistic bullshit! If you want a fucking slave, a bowing barefoot pregnant housekeeper and fuck toy, then you can all go to hell! I am not that kind of woman." She walked out of the room and headed toward the back sitting area as her blood felt as if it were boiling.

She paced back and forth. She couldn't hear their discussions, and then suddenly she sensed the figure in the doorway. She turned around, prepared to give whomever it was hell when she saw Vanderlan.

His eyes were glowing red, his heart pumped faster, and she felt the blood flow through her veins.

"You will do what you are told," he stated, and she held her tongue.

"You don't deserve a response."

He raised his eyebrows at her.

"What?"

"You blocked me before when I sensed your uneasiness about being around all the wolfmen."

"I had no such feelings."

"Liar!" she blurted out.

He took a step closer, unfolding his arms and looking her over. Her flesh tingled and her feminine parts became aroused.

"You must learn to trust our judgment."

"You must learn to trust mine."

"I'm not going to battle like this with you. What I say is final. It's the way."

"Maybe centuries ago, but not for a modern woman like me. It's time to readapt."

He raised his eyebrows at her.

"I never thought I would have a mate, never mind one with a tongue of fire."

"If you prefer easy women, then the gods have surely played a joke on you."

He showed his fangs and made a sound. All he was missing was the black cape lined in red silk, and a pasty white complexion.

Her pussy clenched and her nipples hardened as he swooped toward her. She stepped back only to be lifted into the air. He pinned her against the wall and claimed her mouth in a fierce, primal manner. His fangs bit into her tongue and mouth, and she tangled with him in response. A fire warmed her blood, and as she attempted to control his moves and give as good as she was getting, he used those special vampire powers to restrain her with his mind.

Her arms remained by her side, palms flat against the wall. Her legs were slightly parted as he stepped back and stared at her. She held his gaze and no matter how hard she tried to resist his control, she failed.

"Mine." One by one, the buttons to her blouse snapped open, parting against her skin. Her heart pounded inside of her chest, and her pussy begged to be free from the confinements of her panties and pants. As if on cue, the zipper rolled down, and somehow her pants lowered off of her.

Her eyes widened in shock as Vanderlan's gaze bore into her, his mind in complete control.

"This isn't fair," she stated as all clothing disappeared from her body and the feel of his fingers and hands began to caress her from within.

He was teasing her, showing his power over her hungry sexual need and holy fuck did it turn her on. She wanted to rip into him, suck his cock, and bite his neck, something that would make him feel as out of control as she felt right now.

He pulled off his clothes then reached for her, bending down, placing one thigh over his shoulder before he delved into her pussy with his fingers.

She quaked and shook but still remained pinned against the wall. She couldn't move to touch him or do anything but remain plastered against the wall, creaming herself and feeling her orgasm reach its peak.

"Tell me what you want to do to me."

He pumped his fingers into her pussy then lifted his shoulder higher, making her moan in pleasure.

"This isn't fair. You're using my need for you to control me. Release your mind hold and let me touch you back."

"Not unless you promise to behave and to heed your mates' commands and orders. We do this to protect you. It is our job." He continued to stroke her pussy.

She wanted so much, and she knew that they cared, but they were asking her to change everything about herself.

"You will still be the same person. In fact you will be even stronger as we build this bond between us all."

She was about to explode when he stopped his ministrations.

"Hey!"

"Hey yourself. You promised me something."

"What?" she asked as he lowered her leg and stood up. He placed his hands on her shoulders and gently pushed her down. She immediately understood his request as she lowered to her knees, took his shaft into her hands, and licked the tip.

His hold on her head and hair was firm. Vanderlan was a control freak. That was for certain.

Slowly she opened her mouth and took him in, inch by inch.

She began a rhythm as her senses absorbed his musky scent and each hard ridge of his cock. She could feel his blood pumping and his need to bite her, taste her blood, and fuck her hard.

She began to moan and move her hips.

"Not yet. Only when I am inside of you," he scolded, and immediately the sensations stopped. How the hell did he do that?

* * * *

Vanderlan was losing his control. His mate was a sexual goddess and she had him there already. He yanked at her hair, pulled her mouth from his cock, and lifted her up and against the wall. She straddled him, and in one swift thrust he entered her, making her scream.

Over and over again he stroked her tight, wet pussy until the urge and the hunger inside of him lessened. He was penetrating her deeply when he felt her about to explode. She grabbed at him and panted against his shoulder as he thrust against her with his face against her shoulder. He felt his teeth sharpen when he exploded inside of her, rocking his hips as he bit into her and fed from Dani's blood.

She followed suit and bit into his shoulder, taking her fill and licking him clean before she rested against his shoulder.

"Holy fuck." His body swayed.

He slowly pulled out of her and hugged her to him.

He carried her out of the sitting room and straight upstairs to Van's room. There in the doorway was Van, waiting and looking angry and aroused.

There was no exchange of words. He understood Van's need. All the brothers experienced the same sensations that Vanderlan and Dani had just shared. Vanderlan explained to Dani, and she blushed.

He chuckled as he handed her over to Van.

* * * *

Van was filled with such lust and need for his mate he thought that he would go insane. Their lovemaking projected through their thoughts and onto each of them.

Van lifted her up and covered her mouth before he fell to the bed with her between his legs.

He ravaged her mouth and licked and bit against her skin leaving red marks everywhere in his path.

She moaned and grabbed at his hair then thrust her pussy up against him. He was on fire as he pulled from her, breathing heavy and standing so he could remove his pants. His dick was so fucking hard he could hardly get out of his pants.

"Fuck!" he complained and then pushed off his pants and jumped in between her legs. His cock had a mind of its own as he lined up with her sopping-wet pussy and plunged into her.

Dani squeezed her legs around his waist and accepted his fierce invasion with her own out-of-control need. He pumped his hips and fucked her hard. It was wild and erotic.

"My wolf and the man need to claim you. Please tell me if I'm hurting you." He thrust again, hard and deep. She gasped, but it felt so good, and her need seemed to mimic his own.

"Harder, Van, please. Do what you want."

She looked at him, saw his eyes begin to glow, and then his incisors elongated. It almost felt as if his cock grew inside of her and stretched her vaginal muscles farther with every stroke. She lost her breath, tilted her head back, and screamed as the orgasm overtook her. She lifted up and bit into his shoulder, sucking at his blood before releasing and falling back down.

Van roared like an animal and growled, pumping at rapid speed then exploding as he bit into her shoulder.

She felt the burning sensation and then the warm one that always seemed to follow after one of her mates marked her.

"Mine." He rested his head against her shoulder, caressing her as they readjusted their position on the bed.

* * * *

They left her. Dani knew it. She lay there completely satiated, exhausted, content, and all alone. She heard them in her head, telling her that they loved her, that this was for the best, and that they would see her soon. As the panic and the fear that she was truly alone set in, she heard someone clear their throat by the doorway.

She blinked her eyes open, and there was Bently, arms crossed, a smile on his face, and, of course, a twinkle in his eye.

"Hey, sleepyhead, I've been waiting for you." She felt her belly quiver and her heart soar at the sight of him. Bently was a very handsome man. He looked younger than her twenty-six years, but he was oh so experienced when it came to a woman's body.

He joined her on the bed, jumping on top of the sheets and pulling her into his arms. She lay across him and giggled as he caressed her back under the sheets, making his way closer to her ass.

"I've been waiting for you. I was afraid that you wouldn't wake up until the others came back. I wanted some alone time with my mate."

She ran her fingertips across the material of his black T-shirt. The hard surface of muscles below sent tiny electric currents through her fingertips and up her arm.

"What were you planning for us to do while we wait?" she teased, ultimately getting over the fact that Van and Vanderlan obviously fucked her brains out since she wasn't really pissed at all that they excluded her from assisting in the investigation. She was going to have to gain control over that power they had.

"You will learn to accept our control and see it as love and security." Bently began drawing imaginary circles over her lower spine and between her ass cheeks.

She lifted up slightly to look at him. "Son of a bitch, you heard me?" she asked, and he chuckled then gave her lower ass cheeks a squeeze. She felt his fingers graze lower toward her pussy. He had long, thick fingers.

"I especially enjoyed learning that you liked how Van and Vanderlan 'fucked your brains out,'" he teased, and she swatted at his chest as she attempted to pull away from him. That landed her on her back, the sheets over her belly, exposing her breasts, and Bently pressed between her open thighs. He held her hands above her head and stared down at her, smiling.

"It is going to be so much fun teasing you, Dani," he stated, and she tried to move, but his hold was firm. The movement of her body caused her breasts to lift up and push out toward Bently's face.

He lowered just enough to lick across one nipple, making her squirm even more.

"Stop teasing me," she told him, and he leaned down to lick the other nipple before giving it a nip.

"Ouch!"

"You are quite tasty, mate, and I have grown a bit of an appetite since my last meal. What do you say we take a bath together before the others return?"

"Making love in a bath tub, let me see, that sounds kind of messy. Who's going to clean up afterward?" she teased.

"Fucking your brains out in the tub will be messy. That's the plan, isn't it?" he teased back, and she blushed.

"Quit it. That was a conversation with myself, and I normally wouldn't use such terminology, but I was being sarcastic with myself due to the current situation."

"I like sarcasm, especially when it involves you and fucking," he said, flirting with her, as he pressed his hard cock against the sheets that covered her pussy.

She held his gaze. She couldn't help but giggle and feel his playful demeanor surround her and brighten the air.

"Well, Bently, it seems you have your work cut out for you."

"How is that so?" He rolled from between her legs and off the bed then lifted her up and placed her feet on the rug as the sheets fell around her.

"I am better prepared this time than I was before with Vanderlan and Van. They went all Alpha on me and reversed my anger making me want them instead of remembering why I was angry to begin with. I won't be tricked again."

He took her hand and led her toward the bathroom.

"I have you all to myself awhile, so that's all I care about."

He leaned down and kissed her softly on the lips. Her feelings for the men were growing stronger and stronger by the minute. Her life as it was before didn't seem so important. It was an odd revelation.

"Bently?" she whispered as he turned the faucets on and added some bath salts to the tub.

"Yes." He answered so sweetly as he pulled off his shirt and removed his pants. He stood before her, looking delicious and completely all hers.

"I want you to make love to me." She shyly looked away to swallow the lump of emotions in her throat.

A moment later she was in his arms and he was pressing her head against his chest.

"I plan to do exactly that."

He lifted her up and tested the water with his foot before he lowered her into the tub.

"This feels so good," she stated as the hot water eased her sore muscles. The extra large tub was nearly filled with water.

He took position behind her, leaning back against the side before pulling her between his legs with her back against his chest.

He grabbed the soap and began to lather it up in his hands then bathe her. As he came to her shoulders, she moaned, and he did it again then lowered his hands to her breasts to massage them as well.

"Are you sore from earlier?" he asked in a whisper against her ear.

"Not really. This feels good."

"Lift your legs and place your feet soles-down on the other side of my thighs," he told her, and she did as he said as she adjusted her body. His hands soothed down under her arms, over her belly, and right to her pussy. She was spread wide for him. She closed her eyes as he began to draw tiny circles over her pussy lips then press a finger up into her.

"How does that feel?" he asked.

"Good." She pressed her pussy harder against his finger.

"This will feel really good." He pulled the finger from her pussy and reached up to touch a button. A moment later the jets to the Jacuzzi turned on, and one of the jets was lined up in a position that hit her pussy just right.

"Oh." She jerked, and he held her legs wide so she couldn't close them.

"Feel it, baby," he said as the palms of his hands caressed her inner thighs and the pressure of the jet vibrated against her pussy. He inched his fingers closer and parted her pussy lips causing the sensation to beat against her clit.

"Oh damn," she moaned. Dani could feel her whole body getting aroused from the sensations. "I need one of these at home."

He pressed his finger up into her pussy, making her moan again. "You won't need one. You can use this one whenever you want."

He continued to stroke her pussy, making her thrust her hips upward to meet him.

"So every time I'm in need of pleasure, I can bathe in here and turn on these magical jets and get off?" she teased as she absorbed the sensations.

A moment later he lifted her up, turned her around, and lined his cock up with her pussy. He pressed her down and she took him inside her, grabbing onto Bently's shoulders for support.

"Oh!"

"I think every time you're hungry and aroused you should let me know, Dani. You're not allowed to use this tub without me."

He thrust up and down, the water spilled over the sides, the jets continued to vibrate around her, and now in this position that one amazing jet was stimulating her ass.

"Oh God, I love this tub," she moaned, and he pulled a nipple into his mouth as he continued to thrust up. She helped him by lifting her ass up and down and taking him deep with every movement.

His hands caressed her hips and then her ass. He pulled her against his chest then pressed a finger between her ass cheeks. She pressed back as she lifted up and down onto his shaft. She took over making love to Bently, and he held her steady as her breasts lifted up and down.

"So fucking beautiful. Ride me, Dani, show me how much you like the feel of my cock inside of you."

She absorbed his words, and like an obedient mate, she took control and thrust harder, faster, until she was about to explode.

"I'm coming, baby. Come with me." Bently pressed his finger through her tight rings, and Dani screamed her release as she lowered her face against his shoulder and bit into his skin. Bently did the same, biting her shoulder as he pumped his hips and then exploded inside of her.

They calmed their breathing and remained there until one of them had the energy to move.

Chapter 14

"Son of a bitch, Angus, I don't like this one bit. We send Baher and Miele in there and the crew is gonna know that Task Force One is onto something," Van stated.

"Who gives a shit? If the rogue is in there or any other guilty party, then we'll smoke them out. There's more were in there than human as is," Angus stated.

"Hey, Quinn, any info on who the owner of Cysure Corp is?" Angus asked his brother, who sat in the back of the black truck typing away on the keyboard.

"Not yet but working on it. Whomever it is they really want to remain hidden."

"I say we go in and check it out. Send in Baher, Miele, Adrian and Brady. You and I can take the back entrance," Angus stated.

"Okay. Everyone knows what to do. Let's move," Van said, and they began to head out in various directions and enter the club.

"There are spotters on the rooftop," Vanderlan chimed in through their newly established telepathic link.

"Thanks. Can you handle it?" Van asked.

"Give me five minutes," Vanderlan replied, and Van looked at Angus.

"Spotters on the roof. Vanderlan is handling it."

"Fuck, tell me it isn't so? You hear him in your head, too?"

Van nodded.

"You're going to have to let me in on some of those hidden vampire secrets," Angus teased.

"Be happy he's one of the good guys."

"I'm happy I'm not mated to the same woman as a bloodletter." Angus teased.

"Tell him, I heard that and payback's a bitch."

Van chuckled. "He said payback's a bitch."

"You need to learn to not repeat in your head what other people are saying."

"What fun would that be?"

"There's our cue. Let's move."

* * * *

The music was blasting and the club was crowded as Baher, Miele, and Randolph made their way around the place. "I don't like this. We've got people looking us up and down," Randolph stated to his brothers.

"Let's hit the side door and get out of here." Miele led the way. Through their mind link, they informed their brothers.

As they exited the building, they heard some commotion to their left. Just then a set of five men, wolves from the scent of them, approached.

"What are you doing around here?" one asked.

"What's it to you?" Baher asked.

"Nothing because you'll be dead in a minute." A series of growls echoed around them as numerous wolves attacked at once.

It was mayhem as the men defended themselves against an attack. On the rooftop, Vanderlan was fighting his own battle with a group of wolves. Van and Angus joined him moments later.

In the distance, they heard a larger, deeper growl, and then Baher saw Brady and Adrian shift into wolves and chase one wolf down the alleyway.

It was an intense moment, and as the fighting ceased, both the Fagan and the Fennigan Pack came out on top.

"Is everyone okay?" Van asked as he, Vanderlan, and Angus came down from the rooftop.

"I think I've got a problem," Miele stated. He lay on the ground holding his chest as blood seeped from his wound.

"Fuck. It didn't heal when you shifted?" Van asked, kneeling down on the ground near his brother.

"Silver," Miele whispered as he began to shake.

"Let's get him out of here," Angus stated, and they quickly lifted Miele up and headed back to the truck.

* * * *

Dani held on to Bently as they waited by the front door. They knew that Miele was injured and the men were headed this way. Dani called Margo, who told her what to do.

As the men arrived, carrying a very pale-looking Miele into the house, she covered her mouth and gasped. In her experience as a homicide detective, she had seen many dead bodies and many victims before their last dying breath, and Miele didn't look like he would survive. Something in her leaped into action.

"Get him to the bedroom down the hallway."

Van carried Miele in that direction.

She followed with the others close behind her.

Van set his brother down on the bed and pulled the cloth from his shoulder.

"It's silver, Daniella." Van swallowed hard.

"Shit. I'm not sure what to do. Margo tried to explain, but then she said it would just happen so I'm scared," Dani admitted.

Vanderlan placed his hands on her shoulder. "You can do this. It's why the gods have chosen you for us. You are our protector, too."

She took a deep breath and stared at Miele. There was so much blood and a stench of something that had to be silver lingering around the room.

"Do you smell that?" she asked, and they shook their heads.

"None of you can smell that scent? It's familiar, yet I'm not sure where I recognize it from." Dani dismissed that thought to focus on Miele.

She brushed the hair from his forehead and leaned down closer to him.

"Miele, I have you. I am here now." He moaned then tried to open his eyes. In his mind, he spoke to her.

"Dani, I love you. If I die, know that I love you."

"Shh... now, don't be silly. I'm here, baby. I'm going to try to help you."

Dani placed her hands over the sticky, smelly stuff that oozed from his wound. She allowed the sensations to travel through her hands, up her arms, and into her heart.

Miele. She imagined him in her mind. Cute, light brown hair, hazel eyes as he stood by the stove cooking, trying to get dinner ready. He was nonstop, always on the move. He lived to please and provide for his brothers and for her.

I love you. Return to me whole.

She felt the vibrations travel up her arm, the poison from the silver went through her blood and behind her. Vanderlan gasped then grabbed onto her.

"What is it? What's wrong?" Van asked as the others gathered around.

"I feel it. She's taking in the silver and the pain. Holy shit, it's incredible and weakening even to me." Vanderlan slowly lost the fight to stand and lowered to one knee. He kept his hand on her leg as she continued to heal Miele. A few seconds later and Miele's eyes popped open, he gasped for air as Dani lowered to the floor. She laid her head on his lap and closed her eyes as she tried to gain her strength back.

"Dani? Are you okay?" Randolph asked as he bent down next to her. She opened one eye.

"Miele, is he okay?" She was concerned for him.

"He's awake," Van stated next to her.

"Good. I just need to rest a bit."

Vanderlan stood up and shook the fatigue from his body. "That was amazing." Randolph lifted Dani up, carried her to the other side of the bed, and laid her down beside Miele.

"She's a healer, and if the gods sent her to us as our mate, I fear there are more times like this to come," Van stated, and Bently nodded.

* * * *

"So it was definitely Task Force One. We have the surveillance video. They also have been checking into the company Cysure Corp," Dismar told Marfur as he met with him at his office.

"That is not good. They could figure out our plan to take over their territory."

"Exactly, Marfur. So when will this other rogue and his crew be ready to attack?" Dismar asked.

"Everything is in motion. We have been doing some investigating of our own. It appears that Detrix caught the scent of a human female. She is the one we're looking for. I've got men locating her now and men following Detrix. If we have to take Detrix out ourselves, then we will," Marfur stated confidently.

"Well, at least one of the Task Force members is dead. They also gained some help from the Fennigan Pack. I don't know why they can't stay out of the country and leave us to our business," Dismar stated.

"Not sure, but I'll get an update on their location soon."

Just then, Marfur's phone rang.

He spoke a few moments then disconnected the call.

"Well, the one Fagan Pack member is still alive. We haven't heard differently."

"What? How could that be?"

"Not certain, but interestingly enough, Detrix is nearby the location and the woman he is after is staying there. By the activity, my men believe she may be their mate."

"Son of a bitch! Who is she?" Marfur asked.

"They're working on her name. She's a detective with the police department. She was working the case."

"She's more important than their mate. She has something that is appealing to Detrix."

"But what?"

"Catch her and we'll find out."

"This might not be so easy. If she's their mate, then the chances of taking her are slim to none."

"Try it. Succeed in it, because we need to ensure our plan pulls through."

* * * *

"Dani," Miele whispered as he caressed his mate's cheek gently, moving the hair from her cheeks. She looked like an angel sleeping next to his side. Considering that he was shot with silver, he wasn't in much pain. He felt more bruised than anything serious, and he owed that to Dani.

He caressed her lower lip, absorbing her perfect features. Her lips were pink and plump, her chin firm, and her cheekbones high. She had come to mean so much to him instantly, and the fear of losing her caught hold of his thoughts.

"I love you, Miele. Do not worry. I'm not going anywhere."

He snuggled closer to her then pulled her against his side as he faced her. She wedged her thigh between his legs.

He leaned down and kissed her cheek and then kissed her lips. Placing his hand under her chin and against her neck, he tilted her up toward him so he could gain better access to her mouth.

She moaned against his tongue as he tasted her and made love to her mouth.

She slowly pressed her hips against his groin, and his cock hardened and grew with need to be inside of her.

He released her lips.

"I want to make love to you. I need to feel you. Take off your clothes." He knew he sounded demanding and bossy, but he was doing everything he could to maintain control and not roll her to her back, rip her clothes from her body, and plow into her pussy.

She opened her eyes and began to move around, removing her clothing like he was removing his own. They were naked moments later as he pulled her to him and hugged her tight. Miele needed to feel that skin-to-skin contact with his mate. Dani provided comfort and security, and he hoped he provided her with the same.

He rolled her to her back and shifted his body so he was between her legs, kneeling on all fours above her with his cock at her entrance ready to make love to her.

He stared at her a moment.

Miele thought about the night's events and about Dani.

"I could have died tonight. The thought of never seeing you again hurts so badly inside."

Dani reached up and placed her hand against his cheek. He turned slowly and kissed her palm.

"I love you, Miele, please make love to me now. I need you, too."

He bowed his head and took a deep breath. As he released it, he pressed his cock forward, penetrating her in one smooth stroke. They moaned together, tilting their heads back as her body adjusted to his girth.

"I'm so hard and so needy, Dani. I need so much."

"Take from me, Miele. I want you to take what you need from me, now."

He leaned down so his mouth was inches from her own as he thrust his hips against her. With every stroke, he gained the feelings of safety and control back. Dani did that for him. She provided a safe haven, a place where he could be free from danger or harm and relish in the gift of love the gods had granted to him.

He kissed her mouth and nibbled on her bottom lip then rose above her and increased his speed.

She caressed his forearms and raised her thighs so he could penetrate deeper at an even better angle.

"So beautiful. Fuck, baby, I want to stay like this inside of you forever."

He caressed her breasts as he tilted his hips pressing in and out of her.

He pinched her nipples, making her moan and wiggle beneath his body.

"So sexy." He caressed her arms and clasped her fingers with his own, holding them above her head.

Her breasts pushed upward and her pelvis counterthrust against him as they stared into one another's eyes.

He liked making love to her like this, with her arms above her head in such a submissive position.

"Mine," he growled as he increased his speed. The bed creaked and moaned. Her thighs tightened against his hips as he pushed deeper. He could feel her insides tighten and grasp his cock.

"I'm almost there, baby. Come with me, Dani. Come with me now." He pumped his hips a few more times before he exploded inside of her. He poured himself into her, and he bit her shoulder, marking her his woman. She bit into his shoulder as well. The deep emotions and feelings consumed him as he lay atop her, panting for air before rolling to his side with her against his chest.

Chapter 15

"If I'm going to be staying here a while longer, I'll need some things from my apartment." Dani took a bite from a piece of carrot. She, Van, Vanderlan, Bently, and Baher were in the kitchen. Randolph was hanging out with Miele in the living room, and the Fennigan Pack was out hunting.

"Write down what you need, and Randolph and I can go get the stuff," Bently stated.

"No. That is not going to work. I have things there I need. It's my home." Dani stepped away from the counter.

"This will be your home. We can have some associates move your things in a matter of hours," Van stated.

"I want to go to my apartment and move my own things. I know what to take and what not to take. I have a gun closet that needs to be moved here and secured. Anyone could break in there and steal my stuff."

Vanderlan pulled her to him as he sat on the stool. She was now between his open thighs, and he cupped her face between his hands.

He stared into her eyes.

"You belong here. It is too dangerous."

"You take me, then. You and Van take me there so I can grab what I need. Or bring everyone. I really don't care, but I need stuff." She raised her voice, and he gave her that look of his that warned her to behave.

She took a deep breath and tried to relax. They loved her. She knew that.

"Please. You can come with me."

"Van and I will discuss it and let you know."

She felt her heart drop into her belly. At least it felt that way. Was this how her life was going to be forever? Was she a prisoner in more ways than they could understand?

"No, you are not a prisoner. You are our mate and we protect what is ours." Vanderlin kissed her softly on the lips.

He turned her around and wrapped one arm around her waist so she leaned against his front.

Van stared at her in warning.

"We will give you a decision shortly."

* * * *

He knew who she was now, the one with that unique smell that had gotten away. His wolf craved her. It wanted to be close to her, touch her, cut her, suck from her blood. He needed it more and more every day. Just a hint of her scent sent his wolf into turmoil and desperation. But now he'd found her again. She was guarded by Alpha wolves. The same wolves whose pack he was sent to destroy. The same group of wolves about to be killed, ambushed by another rogue wolf created by Dr. Evans. Well, not before he had a chance at her. Detrix wanted her blood. Just a taste, just to hold her and know that she was his for a few moments. He was obsessed. He knew it and he knew that she would be the death of him, and he didn't care. He needed her, and tonight he would have her.

* * * *

Vanderlan, Van, Baher, and Randolph accompanied Dani to her apartment complex. Miele and Bently remained behind.

She climbed the staircase along with Vanderlan and Van while Randolph kept the SUV running out front. Baher led the way, being sure to check the hallway and then her door and apartment.

"Shit," he exclaimed, and Dani shoved between Van and Vanderlan, two massive figures, in order to see what had gotten Baher upset.

"Oh man, are you kidding me!" she exclaimed as she walked into a major mess. Her place had been ransacked and destroyed.

"I can smell the wolves. Numerous ones have been here. We need to go." Van reached for her hand.

"No. Wait a minute. I have things here. I hid stuff and there's the gun case. If guns are missing, I'll have to report them."

"Where are they? I'll look first," Baher asked, and she told him where to search in her bedroom. The growling sound filled the walls and penetrated through them. She jumped back just as two wolves shoved through the room from the hallway.

Vanderlan shoved her farther into the room and straight into what appeared to be the same wolf that attacked her.

The beast reached for her and she kicked at his sharp claws. The men growled and half shifted. She no longer knew who was who as she circled the room trying to maintain distance from the monster.

It leaped for her and grabbed her as it half shifted back. There were bodies flying around the room and more terrifying roars, but those were drowned out as her own fear gripped her every thought.

"Mine." It snarled. Then she felt its tongue lick across her neck and shoulder. It did that twice and on the third time, she felt its teeth scrape her skin.

"No. Leave me alone," she told it and the arm squeezed against her rib cage, making her lose her breath.

"Mine," it repeated.

"Let her go. She doesn't belong to you," Van stated firmly as he and Vanderlan stood in front of her. Vanderlan's eyes glowed red, and she could sense the force within him. He was trying to control the monster holding her.

"Please, I don't know what you want. What is it you need?" she asked.

"You. Mine," it repeated then began to step backward and farther away from Van and Vanderlan. The floor creaked and immediately the monster turned just as Baher approached. He was attempting to sneak up on them and failed.

She could sense her men's anger and fear for her life. She needed to do something. They couldn't move without him hurting her further.

"I can help you if you need it," she told the beast as it moved around the room and near the doorway.

"Come with me." He squeezed tight. "I taste you now." He licked across her neck making her sick with disgust. She felt his teeth against her skin then the pinch as her blood appeared.

"No! Let her go," Vanderlan commanded, and the beast stopped licking from her bite and instead stared straight at Vanderlan.

"Let her come to me. Release her now." Dani felt the monster ease his hold. If she got the chance, she was going to kill it. She knew that it wanted her. It squeezed her so tight she lost her breath and began gasping for air.

"I can't breathe."

"No!" Baher roared from the side of her, making the wolf restraining her turn toward Baher. Baher shifted into a large brown wolf and swung a huge paw at the wolf's head. The wolf lowered, causing Baher to miss. He eased up his hold, and she bent down, pulled the gun from her ankle, and held on tight. The wolf twisted the other way, causing her other arm to slam down against the ground. She screamed in pain as a series of growls echoed through the room. She sensed the large shadows around her, the beast threw her to the ground, causing her back and shoulders to slam against the floor. She was stunned a moment and then saw the teeth and the beast about to rip her throat out. Pointing her gun straight at its head, she pulled the trigger. One, two, three shots, and she closed her eyes as the beast landed on top of her, its claws scratching her torso.

* * * *

It was complete chaos. The Fennigan Pack arrived to secure the area and intercept the human police. They cleared the room of the numerous dead bodies now in human form. Daniella looked stunned and hadn't said a word to them. She was drenched in blood from the rogue wolf. They each saw her get slashed by the beast. They saw her body slam down onto the floor. Van wasn't certain she would survive it until he saw her injuries heal before his own eyes.

"Daniella. Daniella, baby, look at me. He's gone, honey. You shot him and he's dead," Van stated. Vanderlan gently touched her hands where she still held the gun. He caressed her fingers. "Release the weapon, mate. We have you now." She stared at him a moment.

"I may need it," she replied, and they chuckled.

"Not now you don't. There are more of us than there are of them. It's over, Daniella," Van said as Vanderlan gently tugged the gun from her fingers.

"Talk to me. What hurts?" Van asked.

She looked down at her clothing. It was torn and covered in blood.

"Oh God, did it get me?" she asked.

Van placed his palm against her cheek.

"No, honey. You fought it off and shot it. You did awesome."

She stared at him and crunched her eyes.

"Help me up," she stated, and they each took an arm and assisted her.

"Whoa." Her body swayed. "I feel dizzy."

"She hit her head pretty damn hard when he slammed her to the floor," Vanderlan stated, and she looked at him.

"How the hell am I not dead?" she asked as more voices filled the room. They looked up and saw Eagan and Quinn Fennigan.

"We need to move. Zespian is keeping the regulars at bay," Quinn informed them.

"I need clothes," she stated and Baher approached.

"I grabbed a bunch of stuff that wasn't ripped to shreds. That thing had been stalking the place," Baher stated.

"Take off your shirt and take my shirt." Van removed his shirt. Vanderlan helped Dani lift her shirt off of her and toss it to Quinn.

"Nice," Eagan whispered as he stared at Daniella. Van, Vanderlan, and Baher growled low.

Eagan put his hands up and stepped away chuckling.

"Lucky bastards," Quinn added as Van placed his shirt over Daniella's head and covered her up.

Van lifted Dani up into his arms.

"Everything good in here?" Zespian asked as he entered the room.

All eyes were upon him.

"We're good and heading out now. Meet us at the estate," Van told his uncle.

"Will do." Zespian stared at Vanderlan a moment. Van got a funny feeling in his gut but ignored it as Danielle snuggled against his chest.

* * * *

The men surrounded her when she arrived home. Her need to be close to them, to be touched and caressed by them, was overwhelming, but she knew she needed to shower. Blood stains covered her skin, and her head still felt fuzzy. Her shoulders and back ached, and she was wiped out.

"You're exhausted. Let Baher take you upstairs and help you shower and change. The Fennigan Pack and Zespian will be arriving soon to discuss the case and what happened. After tonight this should be over." Van kissed her softly on the lips. He passed her to Baher, and she snuggled up to his shoulder. He carried her away from the living room and upstairs.

* * * *

"Will she be okay, Van?" Miele asked as they all gathered around the kitchen.

He ran his fingers through his hair and stared at Vanderlan a moment. "It was a close fucking call."

"Too fucking close," Randolph chimed in as he stared at Van. Van wondered if Randolph blamed him. He had given in to Dani's demand to go home and get stuff.

"She's tough. And she's really good with guns. If she had hesitated a moment, she would have been killed by that thing," Vanderlan stated and all eyes fell upon him. He looked at them.

"She was something else. I swear I thought the worse, too, and then the way that thing shifted and licked her." Van shook his head.

"He definitely had my tainted blood in him. I smelled it, sensed it, and when it bit Daniella to take a taste of her, I felt it." Vanderlan banged his fist on the table.

Randolph placed his hand on Vanderlan's shoulder.

"It wasn't your fault. These people who did this stole from you, and because Dani's so tough and street smart, she survived."

Van grew a little angry.

"You blame me for this don't you?" Van asked Randolph, and Randolph stepped away from Vanderlan and gave Van a dirty look.

"She is our mate and we are her Alphas. She's to obey us, not play us. You should have denied her going there. We could have taken her shopping and a few of us could have gone to her apartment and gotten those guns of hers." Randolph ran his fingers through his hair and exhaled.

"I did what I felt was right. We've taken her away from everything she knows. She's a homicide detective and a strong woman, I gave in a little, thinking that we had her covered. In the end, she saved herself because of her skills," Van admitted then turned away from them.

"This all doesn't matter now. The rogue is dead. Let's wait for Zespian to arrive and go over the situation. The Fennigan Pack covered up the mess and Quinn has information, too. Clear our heads and get back to business. Daniella is safe and right upstairs with Baher," Bently added, and they were all silent.

* * * *

Baher gently undressed Daniella as the shower water heated up.

She looked tired and her eyes were glazed over, but her pupils weren't dilated. He had wondered if she suffered a concussion from the attack after hearing about the incident at her apartment.

"You sure you can stand up okay? You still feel dizzy?"

"I'm feeling better, Baher. I just want to get this blood off of me," she told him, and he smiled.

He stripped his clothes off and walked her toward the walk-in shower.

He watched as she maneuvered under the spray of water and moaned as the heat hit her skin.

"Too hot?" he asked with concern.

"No, just right," she stated in a gurgling sound as she spoke under the spray of water.

She ran her hands through her hair, and he grabbed the soap, lathering it up to help wash away the blood.

It took a little while to remove any signs of the attack, and he got sidetracked more than a few times as he caressed some parts more than others.

"You're beautiful, Dani." He leaned down to kiss her lips.

Dani reached up and embraced him, pulling him against her hard, and making her back hit the wall behind her. She moaned and he tried to pull away, but she apparently had a different idea.

"I need you, Baher. I need you inside of me, please."

"I need you, too. I was worried."

He lifted her up, and she spread her legs, straddling his waist as he maneuvered against her.

His cock was hard, his beast still uneasy about how close she came to death tonight.

She grabbed his shoulders and tilted her pelvis up so he could align his cock with her entrance.

"Easy, baby, I don't want to cause more bruises."

"You won't. I need this. I need you." She held his gaze. Her light-green eyes lit up his heart as he pressed his cock up into her pussy. Wet strands of her long brown hair clung to her shoulders. Her vaginal muscles clung tight to his shaft, taking his breath away. Once fully inside of her, she held him tight, making it difficult for him to move. She kissed his neck and inhaled deeply against his skin.

He pulled his hips back then pressed forward slowly into her. She continued to cling to him and hold him tight. Tonight had scared her. It was obvious, but she was a tough one. Dani and her guns. She would have died without it tonight. Thank God she was insistent on bringing it with her.

She eased up her hold enough for him to increase his thrusts. She leaned back against the shower wall and he caressed down her breasts to her hips. He squeezed her hip bones and watched her large breasts bounce with every thrust into her.

She held his shoulders and counterthrust against him as they locked gazes.

"Harder, Baher, please," she asked, and he obliged, taking her hard against the wall as the spray of water enveloped them.

Over and over he thrust his hips. His cock grew harder and thicker inside of her as she moaned and called his name.

He reached one hand up and pinched her nipple, sending her over the edge. She screamed his name, and he pressed his chest against hers, their mouths landing on the other's neck as they exploded together while biting into the other's skin.

"That was amazing." He tried to calm his breathing.

"I feel so weak," she whispered, and he slowly pulled back and stared into her light-green eyes.

"I love you, Daniella. I was so worried about you." He kissed her softly on the lips as he eased out of her and lowered her feet to the shower floor.

"I love you, too." She told him then pressed kisses against his chest, over his heart.

Chapter 16

Baher insisted on carrying her downstairs to the living room. He wouldn't allow her to walk after noticing how stiff and achy she was.

"There she is," Vanderlan stated as Baher let her down. Vanderlan pulled her into his arms to kiss her then snuggle next to her neck. She inhaled deeply, trying to absorb as much of him as she could. It comforted her and made her feel safe whenever one of her men held her in his arms. It was such an intense feeling she almost felt like the odd ball out and clingy. They may not like that. She tried to pull back, but Vanderlan wouldn't allow it. Maybe they felt just like she did and they needed to hold her for reassurance.

"We feel it, too. The need to be as close as possible to our mate. Clingy is a good thing." He kissed the bridge of her nose.

She smiled up at him then cringed a little as he released her. Vanderlan scrunched his eyebrows together.

"You're hurt?" he asked, and the others approached with concern for her.

"I'm here with all of you and I am fine. Tired, a little achy, yes, but fine."

Van remained a bit farther away from the others, and she had recalled hearing some of their conversation earlier. It seemed that Randolph was a bit upset with Van for allowing her to go to her apartment.

She walked over toward Randolph and took his hand into her own. Standing up on tiptoes, she kissed him, and he hugged her to him tightly. He inhaled against her hair and caressed her back and then her ass, giving it a squeeze.

She chuckled.

"Come with me." She took his hand while the others watched.

Van had his arms crossed in front of his chest. He stared at them and at her with a mix of emotions. The vibes she got off of him were powerful. He felt to blame and he wasn't. While still holding Randolph's hand, she reached for Van's and took it, raising it to her mouth and kissing the top of it. His demeanor changed from one of anger and guilt to calmness. He reached out and caressed her cheek. She turned into it to kiss his palm.

"Enough with being angry with one another. You are brothers, we are all mates, and what happened tonight was no one's fault. We were dealing with a rogue wolf and it all worked out. He's dead and we're all together. So, enough." She pulled their hands together with her own.

She hugged Van, and Randolph hugged her back, and she sensed them nodding at one another in acceptance of what she told them.

"I'd like some loving from my mate, too, you know," Miele chimed in and she pulled from Van and Randolph to go to Miele and Bently. They each hugged her then sandwiched her between them.

Her stomach growled and they laughed.

"Come on, mate, I made some sandwiches for all of us." Miele took her hand, and she hugged his forearm to her chest.

* * * *

They were eating when the Fennigan Pack arrived along with Zespian. Dani was sitting on a stool near Vanderlan, who was holding her hand. As Zespian entered, everyone said hello and greeted him. Dani felt his eyes upon her, and Vanderlan squeezed her hand then tried to cover up his move by moving their hands along her legs.

She was wearing a pair of shorts and a T-shirt, and as his cold hand caressed her thigh, she shivered. Randolph sat on the stool beside her and placed his hand on her thigh as well, seeping warmth into her skin.

She had a funny sensation inside, and then her mind was blocked from Vanderlan's emotions.

She stared at him, trying to get him to look at her, but he didn't as Zespian entered the room and greeted the other men.

"So, what's the latest update?" Van asked as the Fennigan men grabbed food to eat and beers from the refrigerator.

Quinn took a slug of beer then began to talk as he placed the bottle down on the island in the kitchen and opened up his laptop. Dani looked at the screen and an insignia of Cysure Corp with a blue globe in the center and stars and pinpoints on the globe covering it. It was a catchy image and made her think international company.

"Cysure Corp is an international company that owns hundreds of businesses. It's huge, so huge of an operation it has millions of employees," Quinn began to say.

"Who is the owner?" Vanderlan asked, and Dani caught his gaze shift to Zespian, and as she looked at Zespian, he remained staring at her. She felt her blood begin to hum with awareness. *What the fuck?*

"Calm down, Daniella, it is not what you think. Just relax. He is not an enemy."

"What is he to me, then? I feel some sort of connection to him, yet, I don't even know who he is."

"With time, Daniella," Vanderlan told her through their mind link, and she pulled her hand away from his in frustration.

Randolph's hand on her thigh tensed a moment, and then he began to caress her softly.

"So I had to do a lot of digging. It was hours of digging, and interestingly enough I found out that Cysure Corp, over the last five years, has been financially supporting a private medical facility under the care of Dr. Evans. He is a human. However, his associate, Lemlock Porter, a London scientist with the Claiborne Pack, is involved along with Marfur Cartright," Quinn stated.

"Marfur Cartright? Isn't he a commander to Dismar, an elder of the circle?" Van asked.

"Sure as shit he is. It appears, through further investigation, that the Cartright Pack and Dismar himself want to take over your territory and your pack. One of my informants gave me the heads up. He's got a man working undercover in Cysure. There's been some buzz about a special experiment, but only a handful of individuals are involved. I am assuming it has something to do with the rogue wolf Dani killed. Your land is a phenomenal and strategic piece of property. Though small, the Fagan Pack contains all the characteristics and special individuals to maintain power. Now, with Daniella here being a healer, she adds to the bonus package," Quinn told them.

"Fuck! That piece of shit is a damn elder, and he's planning this type of treason? We need to inform the other leaders. We need to speak with someone of authority on this matter before he tries something else, besides this rogue wolf Daniella killed," Van stated firmly.

"We need to gather further evidence then make arrangements to speak with elders who can be trusted. We should contact Samantha, the Valdamar Pack, or Lord Crespin. They have been trying to weed out the evildoers, even those connected to the circle," Angus stated.

"It won't be a problem to get Valdamar's assistance in this. Samantha will definitely want to meet with Daniella, and she'll send any necessary help you all need to maintain control of what is Fagan territory," Zespian added.

Dani felt the same thing inside of her as Zespian felt. It was just a minor feeling, like recognition, and it came from Vanderlan.

She used her mind to seek more answers when she felt the gentle caress of a finger against her cheek. She blinked her eyes and absorbed the fact that she was next to Van and he hadn't moved a muscle.

Vanderlan.

She looked at him, and he wasn't even looking at her, yet she felt him again caress her cheek. She knew it was him and her entire body warmed.

The conversation continued around her as she stood up and slowly walked toward Vanderlan. But instead of stopping near him, she walked toward the refrigerator and right by Zespian.

Vanderlan tensed a moment, and she felt his eyes upon her and so were Zespian's.

She took a sip of water then placed the glass into the sink. With Zespian inches away from her, she felt an awareness flow through her veins. Her blood moved a little quicker or perhaps identified with something in the surrounding environment.

"We'll notify all pack Alphas of the situation and to remain on guard for any potential attacks," Van stated, and Dani looked at him from across the kitchen. The conversation seemed to end, and some of the Fennigan Pack stood up as everyone conversed.

"You did an excellent job, Daniella. I wouldn't have expected anything less. It is an honor to have you as part of the Fagan Pack. Many will be thrilled as they hear of your existence." Zespian bowed his head then lifted back up to smile at her.

He was a very nice man, and she felt his sincerity, but she also heard the bit of nervousness in his voice and even saw the tension in his body.

He stared into her eyes, and she held his gaze. There was something there. Some kind of connection.

"Did we ever meet before that night at the crime scene? I mean at the department or something, because I don't recall ever meeting you yet, something about you is so familiar."

He looked as if he were about to answer when his eyes changed from an awareness and brightness to a bit of fear, she thought, as Vanderlan wrapped his arms around her from behind.

She felt her mind go fuzzy, the need to interrogate Zespian disappeared, and instead she absorbed the feeling of being in

Vanderlan's arms and feeling his embrace as his body remained against her.

"I think it's time to call it a night, Daniella. Zespian, as always, it is good to see you and have you on board to assist your nephews."

"Yes, Vanderlan, I am proud of their accomplishments and happy that they, and you, have found your mate. I will do anything I can to assist in the protection of all." Zespian bowed his head then walked away.

Daniella found the short conversation strange, and then she felt Vanderlan begin to walk her out of the kitchen and toward the other room. As they made it to a spare bedroom down the hallway, he turned her toward him after closing the door behind them.

He cupped her face and head as he pressed her back against the door.

"You must learn to not challenge my control of you, mate."

She stared into his eyes and felt his need to block his thoughts from her. She closed her eyes, feeling a bit distant at the moment. Why was he doing that so much lately?

He covered her mouth with his own and began to kiss her deeply. He explored her mouth with his tongue and pressed his hips against her own. Immediately she felt his cock, and her pussy clenched with need for him.

The feel of his hands against her skin pressed under her shirt and over her breasts before he pulled from her mouth and tore the material from her body.

Next came her shorts and panties before he lifted her up against the solid oak door. Everything in the home was custom made. The doors were thick and solid, yet smooth against her back.

His mouth came down on hers again as he held her with one arm while he undid the zipper to his pants and shoved them down his legs.

Why was he trying so hard to block her and make her curiosity disappear? What was it about Zespian and the sensations she had?

He shoved against her, making her stir a moment as her spine made contact with the door again.

She gripped his shoulders as he moved his lips from her lips to her neck, scraping his teeth across her skin. She could no longer think of anything but Vanderlan's cock inside of her, stroking her pussy and bringing her satisfaction.

He pressed the bulbous top to her pussy and shoved upward, making her lose her breath and grip him tighter. He sucked harder on her neck and began a series of fast thrusts into her, sending her moaning and reciprocating his moves.

She ran her hands up his solid arms and shoulders to his head and hair. She pulled on the locks as she pressed him harder against her, absorbing the stroke of his cock and the teeth against her skin as her need grew stronger.

"Mine," he growled low against her neck, licking, sucking then pressing his teeth harder against the skin, breaking it. She jerked, her body exploded while he continued to fuck her against the door and feed from her blood.

She lost all focus. Her mind embraced the connection between them as Vanderlan exploded inside of her.

She held him to her in the aftershocks of their lovemaking. He panted against her neck and squeezed her tightly.

"I love you, sweet mate. You are more important to me than life itself," he told her. She hugged him back and tightened her legs, which remained locked against him.

His cock stirred, still hard and ready for her again, but his mind revealed his need to help the others plan.

"Through you, I am truly part of the Fagan Pack now. They will need some help and I want to be sure to assist them."

"I know, Vanderlan, and I love you, too," she told him before kissing him softly on the lips.

He pulled from her body and gently settled her feet back onto the floor. They hugged before both of them began to redress.

* * * *

Vanderlan walked down the hallway toward the kitchen when he saw Zespian.

"Congratulations, Vanderlan. She is special."

Vanderlan held Zespian's gaze.

"How long have you known about her?" Vanderlan asked after he looked around to be sure no one was in earshot.

Zespian took a deep breath.

"Not long at all. I mean, I recognized the sensation, or should I say that my blood recognized and identified with hers? It didn't register as anything more than perhaps the thought that you are more caring to the wolf packs than you've let on. You saved my life centuries ago as you saved her parents' lives."

Vanderlan didn't want to talk about that night. He had no idea why he even helped the wolves, just that something stronger, more powerful than his own abilities cleared his mind of any negatives to helping them and forced him to step in. He could only come to the conclusion that those three wolves, Zespian, Farrow, and his mate Clara needed to survive. He never thought for a moment that Farrow and Clara's child, their daughter, would be his mate and that of the Fagan Pack, Zespian's nephews.

"It is quite amazing, the resemblance between Daniella and her mother. Her parents believe her to be dead," Zespian told Vanderlan and he looked shocked. He thought that they had left this realm after being banned from their pack by the elders of Fagan for accepting a vampire's help instead of dying. For centuries, the wolves and vampires were in conflict with one another. His relationship with the Alphas of Fagan Pack, Van, Miele, and Randolph, Bently, and Baher opened up many wolves' minds to assist one another and be allies instead of enemies.

To know that a bond was forming between himself and the pack without his knowledge humbled him.

"The powers of the gods are great. There's a reason for this connection and bond. Will you tell Daniella of her parents?" Zespian asked.

"You say they are not in this realm. Do you know how they parted ways with their daughter?"

Zespian sighed then swallowed hard.

"She was taken from them by a rogue wolf. Someone stepped in and saved her, but the threat was too big to return her to her parents. The fact that she is a healer explains it all. Healers are rare, and the need to protect them until their destiny calls takes precedence over parental love. A young healer, easily manipulated, could wind up in the wrong hands."

"Well, she is where she belongs now, and we are her protectors."

"Her parents will be beside themselves when they learn that she is still alive."

"What?" Daniella asked as she emerged from the hallway.

Vanderlan turned toward her. He was so shocked at learning whose daughter she was and that her parents were alive that he never heard her approach. She did that to him. She weakened the walls of protection he had built over the centuries that had always blocked out the hurtful accusations and insults from those not of the bloodletters.

"Take my hand, Daniella." Vanderlan reached his hand out to her. She hesitated, but he eased her mind and pushed a bit of control over her. She raised her eyebrows at him in defiance that made him smirk inside. She was truly an amazing mate. She was strong-willed, empowered, young, and beautiful.

She took his hand but then looked at Zespian.

"We share the same blood don't we?" she asked him, and Zespian nodded.

"You're not my—"

"I am not your father, but I was good friends with your parents. I knew them well."

"I will explain, come, and let's sit down."

* * * *

"I want the others here. I need them here," she told Vanderlan, and he nodded before she reached out in her mind to her other mates.

They immediately joined them in the living room, and they appeared on guard and concerned.

Bently kneeled down next to her and caressed her thigh.

"Are you okay? Is something wrong?" he asked, and she touched his cheek.

"Vanderlan has some explaining to do." She looked at Vanderlan as Bently took a seat beside her.

"Many centuries ago, Zespian and Daniella's parents were being hunted. They were on the run, trying to get back into their territory, when a group of rogue wolves attacked them. They needed help and despite the negative feelings wolves and vampires shared, I was compelled by a power greater than my own to assist them."

"He shared his blood with the three of us and saved our lives. What he did should have killed him, weakened his abilities, but it didn't. It made us stronger and Vanderlan even more powerful," Zespian stated, and everyone appeared shocked.

"That is why you are able to travel day or night? You're not affected by the sun?" Bently asked.

Vanderlan nodded. "It wasn't only me and my powers. Daniella's parents were mediums. They, in many ways, worked for the gods, getting messages to those in need or in danger. They were being hunted for their powers and abilities. At the time I had no idea what I was doing. I just did what I was compelled to do by the power of the gods. The reason I was compelled to save them has become clearer.

Daniella was to be my mate. She was and is my destiny and yours," Vanderlan stated and everyone began to ask questions.

Vanderlan tried to answer them and so did Zespian. Then Daniella spoke.

"Are my parents still alive?" she asked as she clasped her hands together. Vanderlan felt her sadness mixed with excitement. The trepidation of not knowing if they were alive and then the hope that somehow they were.

He touched her hand.

"They are alive, Daniella. They live in another realm under the protection of the gods," Zespian stated, and she covered her mouth and gasped.

"What do you mean by another realm?"

"There are other realms for other mythical creatures. Places to go and hide or go to rest and live," Zespian told her.

"Like time travel?" she asked.

"Something like that but more mystical and magical," Van stated, drawing her attention toward him.

"My parents can be contacted? They can be sent here to me?" she asked, and Vanderlan looked at Zespian.

"The gods make the decisions. If they remain in danger or perhaps bring danger to you, then they must remain under guard," Van told her.

"But I am bound, mated to a vampire and five Alpha wolves. What danger could I possibly be in now that I've killed the damn rogue?"

"We are not certain. The mating bond is strong and nearly complete. If you are meant to reunite with your parents, then it will happen, Daniella," Van told her, and she sighed.

"To think that all this was hidden from me and so deep that even I wasn't aware that I was more than a human woman. Other realms, spiritual creatures, parents saved by the blood of the vampire I am now mated to, it's all so confusing and outrageous."

"But it is your destiny, and you have the power and ability to handle it all. You are special, Daniella. The more we learn, the more important it is that we strengthen our bond and remain together to fight whatever battles lie ahead," Van stated.

"Well, it seems that we've survived our first battle together and tried out those healing powers I have. Perhaps now is a time to recuperate and rearrange some things for what may or may not lie ahead." She looked at Miele and he smiled.

"We need to finish up our plans in taking down Cysure Corp and help remove Dismar from the circle." Van rose from his seat.

"Well, I'm pretty tired with information overload, so if you all don't mind, I'm going to shower then head to bed. You can fill me in tomorrow morning," she told them then pointed at Van and gave him a firm look.

He in return pulled her up from the couch and into his arms. He kissed her fully on the lips then murmured against her lips.

"You have much to learn, mate," he teased, and she kissed him back before he released her, giving a light tap to her ass as she sashayed away from her men.

Chapter 17

He calmed his breathing. He knew that the wolves were a good distance away from their mate. His master wanted her, and he would be thrilled to know that she was also a healer. Detrix's need to have her cost him his life. He attacked instead of planned. The enforcer knew what to do, and he didn't need any help. He pulled out the syringe, the one that Dr. Evans had given him. It ensured the woman would remain knocked out for a long time. He watched her through the window on the balcony. She was beautiful, and as he inhaled, her unique scent enticed him from beyond the slightly ajar glass doors.

He didn't want to wait any longer. She turned away from him, preparing to undress when he made his move.

In a flash she had no idea what hit her. He struck her in the neck, she fell into his arms as her eyes widened with fear and something else before he lifted her and carried her out onto the balcony. He leaped down over the railing onto the grass and escaped into the night with the treasure in his arms and his mission nearly accomplished.

* * * *

"Daniella!" both Vanderlan and Van stated then jumped from their seats at the dining room table. Everyone scrambled around, running to find her, to track the wolf they immediately sensed the moment they ran outside. "He was here. He took her from the bedroom," Van stated.

"I can't get a response from her," Randolph chimed in as he held his hands against his ears as if that may help to hear her through their link.

"Get on it now," Van ordered as his brothers shifted and took off in the direction the wolf and their mate had gone.

"Gather the Fennigan Pack. We will need their help," Van ordered Vanderlan.

They held one another's gaze.

"He's on a mission from his creator, if it's a lab-created rogue as the others suspect. We need to know the addresses and locations nearby of Cysure," Vanderlan stated.

"I'm on it. Let's move," Van replied, and they headed toward the house.

* * * *

Daniella awoke as she felt the cold, hard object against her skin.

She opened her eyes and locked gazes with a man in a white coat she didn't recognize. She attempted to move her arms, but they were tied to the bedposts with very little slack for her to move.

"Who are you?" she asked, her voice dry as she coughed.

He reached over toward her face and touched her cheek.

"You and I are going to get very close. I've searched for you for so long. I'd nearly given up when out of nowhere you appear like a gift from the gods. They must know that I am destined to rule."

"What the hell are you talking about?" she asked, and he looked angry a moment.

"She is not part of the plan, Evans. You can have her and play with her later. Right now my Alpha needs to strike and take over Fagan Pack territory. The enforcer and the other men are in position. Can we make our move?" another man asked, and the doctor looked back at him.

"They know that your Alpha Dismar is planning a takeover and is responsible for the rogue wolf attacks. They have the Fennigan Pack assisting them and other nearby packs. It's your choice if you would like to commit suicide," Evans told the other man in an angry voice, but then he looked back at Daniella and smiled.

"So beautiful and so full of everything I need to achieve greatness."

He ran the knife across her forearm and smiled.

"I may have to taste your blood myself. I hear that the powers of a healer are great."

Dani could tell that this guy was crazy, but she wasn't sure if what he said was true or not. She also didn't mention that she had vampire blood in her as well.

"Daniella, where are you?"

She heard Vanderlan's voice, and she jerked a moment. The doctor paused before cutting her.

"Afraid of the pain, dear? You'll need to get used to it. I plan on taking many samples of your blood and your flesh. Before long, you'll become immune to being dissected and eventually die."

Fear gripped her insides.

"Help me, Vanderlan, this man is insane."

"Where are you?"

"I have no idea. I'm tied to a bed."

"What?"

"This sick doctor who made the rogue wolves tied me to the bed and is going to take my blood and dissect my body, so if you could help me, that would be great."

"Give us a description of where you are."

"Oh, Dismar and a rogue called 'the enforcer' are going to try to take over Fagan territory right now. This guy here, not sure of his name, is leaving now. They know you all found out about the bad elder. They don't care. They're coming to take over. You need to tell Van."

"I am here, Daniella, but we have others to handle that. Where are you? Describe the location," Van interrupted.

She jerked and yelled as the doctor cut her arm. The blood seeped from her wound, and he began to take vials of her blood. Then he stared at it as she told her men what was happening. She tried to focus on giving a description of her surroundings. There were no windows. There were tables and white walls. It was a sterile environment aside from the bed she was tied to.

She wiggled and attempted to fight his moves.

"Don't move," he yelled, and she described what she saw to her men. Then a sensation and idea formed in her head. She closed her eyes and concentrated as her wound healed before the doctor's eyes.

"Amazing." He cut her again, shocking her.

She healed but it still hurt.

"What do you want from me?" she asked.

"What he can't have." She heard the voice then heard the shot as the doctor fell over and onto the floor.

There in the doorway was a tall man, a wolf, she could tell by the glowing eyes.

"You're coming with me." He walked to the bed and began to undo the ropes she was bound with.

"Who are you?" she asked, and he gripped her tighter as he shoved her forward, making her fall to the hard concrete floor.

She gasped and he grabbed her by her hair to lift her up.

"Let's go," he yelled as she held his hands that gripped her hair so tightly.

"The doctor's dead. Some guy shot him. A wolf, I think, and he's taking me somewhere."

"What does he look like?"

"He's very tall, Van, with dark hair and an ugly, mean face. He's taking me somewhere."

"It could be Marfur. We think we know where you are. Give us descriptions of everything you see."

Just then they entered a hallway and there was a huge logo of Cysure Corp like she saw on Quinn's laptop.

"Cysure. I'm at one of their buildings."

"Keep moving. Dismar doesn't like to be kept waiting."

"He just mentioned taking me to Dismar."

"Excellent. We've got men on him and he's not far from one of the Cysure buildings. It must be where you are. Hold tight and don't do anything crazy, Daniella. We'll get to you," Vanderlan interrupted.

* * * *

The car ride wasn't more than fifteen minutes. The closer they came to their destination the stronger Daniella felt the presence of her men. As they approached what appeared to be a very large estate situated on lots of beautifully landscaped land, she noticed the many men and wolves that seemed to be guarding it. She told her men and they didn't respond.

"Get out." Marfur shoved her from the car, making her fall to the gravel ground.

"Quit doing that!" she yelled at him as he followed her out of the car. He lifted her up by her T-shirt then slammed her against the car, making her lose her breath.

"If I were you, I'd censor that mouth before you meet Dismar. He's older and not so tolerant of disrespect."

He pulled her back toward him then turned her toward the walkway. She felt his hand fist the T-shirt and force her forward. Then she noticed the very large guy with bulging muscles that had driven them. He followed close behind like some goon bodyguard. If he were a wolf, which was quite possible, then he would be a gigantic one.

As they walked into the enormous home, she saw a man descending the large cherrywood staircase. The banister and spindles matched the cherrywood walls and stairs, and she noticed the intricate designs of carved wolves on the posts to both sides of the beginning staircase. It was very ornate and the man descending those stairs appeared high class. His nose was long and rather pointy, almost an odd size. He wore a tailored gray jacket, but underneath was a tight burgundy shirt that stretched across a protruding chest and a slim waist. He was a wolf, and an evil one at that. This was Dismar.

He descended the final two steps and looked her over as if she were an enticing meal. Every feminine instinct placed her body in warning mode. He was not to be trusted. Her cop instincts identified him as criminal, and as he invaded her personal space and inhaled against her neck, she responded like she normally would, wolf or not.

Dani shoved him away only to be grabbed by the throat by the goon behind her.

She lost her breath and her footing.

Dismar chuckled low and deep as he circled around her and continued to take deep breaths. His eyes began to glow.

"I smell them on you, but it won't matter by the time I finish with you."

"Planning on carving me up like your doctor friend?" she replied, and the goon squeezed her throat a little tighter, causing her to stop speaking and try breathing. She hardly caught her breath and pressed her body against him to find some give in his hold.

"I assure you that I don't intend on cutting you up. In fact I believe that most of your time will be spent tied to my bed while I rid you of the scent of such miniscule wolves. You do know that the Fagan Pack will no longer exist when I am through."

She struggled to breathe and respond, and Dismar gave a look to the goon holding her. He slowly released his grip.

"The Fagan Pack will always exist."

"Not without you, a healer. You belong to me now, and you are quite the asset and bonus prize in my plan. But enough small talk." He looked her over and stepped a little closer.

He grabbed her face and held it tight while he looked into her eyes. He was an evil bastard, and she sure wished she had one of her guns right now.

"You'll forget about your men soon enough. Once I get through with you, you'll be bound to me and ready to spread your legs on my beck and call. With your body, I'll be more than satisfied."

She swallowed hard but held her ground. She was tough.

"You're really not my type. Small, cocky, Napoleon complex. I prefer real men, not weaklings like yourself that have to use a goon to control your women."

The goon released her after one eyebrow raise from Dismar.

She relaxed a moment and shifted her shoulders to straighten her shirt. She never expected the punch to her stomach or the way Dismar yanked her hair back and restrained her himself.

"You will learn to be more obedient."

He covered her mouth with his own. He groped her breasts and pulled her nipples hard, making her gasp in pain. She tried to fight him off, but then the goon tripped her up as Dismar released her, and she fell to the marble floor.

Her temper was getting the better of her.

A moment later, alarms began to blare throughout the house. Dani looked around as numerous men shifted into wolves as they passed her. The sight took her breath away as one moment there were men and the next, their bodies changed forms before her eyes and became hairy wolves on four legs.

Marfur returned, looking worried as he passed a gun to the goon. Good. That meant that her men and their pack members were there.

"Remain here. You have the gun with the silver in it," Dismar ordered to the big goon. Marfur bowed his head then took off out the front door.

So the big guy had the silver bullets. Okay, now how to get that gun out of his hands?

"Who are you anyway, and what's with the alarms?" she asked as Dismar stared at her. He grabbed her arm and yanked her to him.

"You are a healer and you now belong to me. Let's go." He yanked her along with him and the goon followed. In the distance, she thought she heard numerous growls and roars of pain. Then she sensed her men and felt their struggle.

"What's going on? Where are you?" she asked them.

"Fighting our way inside with the Fennigan Pack and some of our other pack members. Are you okay?" Van asked.

"I'm with some big goon and Dismar. He thinks I belong to him."

"Not fucking going to happen."

"They have silver bullets. I'm going to try to get the gun away from the big guy."

"No. Remain where you are and we will come help you," Van yelled and then came the others and their commands followed by instant silence.

Dismar shoved her through a doorway to an outside garage area across the grass. She had to do a double take as she saw the multitude of wolves fighting to the death around them. It was outrageous, and she feared for her men.

A moment later, something big and furry jumped in her way and knocked into the big guy. He dropped his gun, and she jumped toward it as Dismar tried to beat her to it.

She saw the big guy shift to a huge ferocious wolf, and then she noticed three other wolves join in.

She immediately knew who they were. Randolph, Baher, and Bently.

They fought the goon and soon others began to surround her and Dismar. She wrestled with him for the gun, and she pulled the trigger shooting Dismar in the neck. Rolling to her side, she still held the gun as another wolf charged her.

"Shoot it, Dani. Shoot whatever you can until you run out of bullets," Randolph told her.

"Where is she? Can you protect her?" Van asked from a distance.

"Dani's got a gun with silver bullets. Probably three more shots left," Randolph stated to Vanderlan.

"Vanderlan and I are on our way!" Van yelled through their link.

Just then, Dani saw another wolf jump on the wolf about to attack her. She had one more bullet. The two wolves fought and she knew that it was Miele. Now Miele, Baher, Bently, and Randolph battled side by side against double the amount of wolves in front of her.

She jumped up, circling, and prepared to fire as she waited for Van and Vanderlan to arrive. There were wolves fighting everywhere, and some seemed to be recovering as if the battle was nearly over. She assumed those wolves were Fagan Pack members. She wasn't sure, since her concern was now for Miele. Miele took a hit to his ribs then retaliated with a swipe of his paw across the enemy's throat. The wolf fell to the ground. Then she saw the big wolf striking her men repeatedly until Randolph, Bently, and Baher attacked at once, killing him on the spot.

She lowered her weapon as Van and Vanderlan came into view. A sigh of relief hit her until she saw them leap as if trying to get to her.

She turned in time to see the large black wolf leap through the air at her. She aimed and fired, hitting it in the head before it landed on top of her, bringing them both to the ground with a thump.

The pain was instant. The large heavy wolf landed on her full force and smashed her body to the ground. Her shoulder blades burned and her spine ached. She couldn't move.

"Daniella! Daniella!" Van yelled as they removed the wolf from her body. She tried to take in air, her lungs felt tight, her ribs felt broken.

"I. Can't. Breathe," she whispered then felt the tears reach her eyes. She was a healer, sent to protect them. Was this it? Was this the moment, the battle that they needed her help for, and now her life was over?

"Stop. No, Daniella, this is not over. Wolves are heavy creatures. He slammed down on top of you. You're injured, but you are not going to die," Miele stated.

"She blinked her eyes and tried not to move a muscle. Everything hurt. She took in the sight of her men, all of them.

Van—her Alpha wolf, dark black hair, his piercing green eyes and skin covered in tattoos—was superior and commanding.

Miele. Oh her nonstop, always busy moving, shaking, jiving Miele. He smiled at her, and his hazel eyes sparkled.

Randolph, her big, bad, serious, man-of-few-words mate. She loved his big muscles, the intricate tattoos on his arms, and his serious dark eyes. He caressed her skin and she felt the tingling move through her battered body.

"Touch me. All of you." She whispered as tears filled her eyes. Through the glossiness she looked to Bently next. Her sexy flirt and jokester, who appeared so serious right now she felt her own heart ache. She turned slightly toward Baher, cringing from the pain a moment until Baher uncrossed his arms, her stubborn, set-in-his-ways wolf, and touched her arm, caressing it. His hazel eyes held hers, understanding and hopefully feeling her connection to him.

The tingling continued and grew stronger.

She looked around, unable to see Vanderlan until she felt him caress her cheeks from above her. He knelt down, her head between his knees. She smiled. A vampire. She was mated to five Alpha wolves and a strikingly handsome vampire with black eyes that turned red with deep emotion and shoulder-length black hair that made him appear sexy and lethal. She was surrounded by every woman's fantasy come true, and she loved them all, individually and together.

"Touch me. Hold me at once and show me you love me as much as I love you," she whispered then closed her eyes as they did as she asked. The warmth flowed through her body, her neck where the star tattoo remained tingled and the pain ached so bad she began to breathe rapidly and wondered if she would die in their arms.

"No. No, Daniella, we need you and love you," Randolph said. She felt the pain and then their love surrounded her as darkness overtook her.

* * * *

"Oh by the gods, no. No, she can't die!" Bently yelled.

Vanderlan checked her pulse then inhaled against her neck.

"She is alive. She's healing. I can feel the connection through our mingling blood. She needs to sleep off the damage done to her body," Vanderlan stated.

"Let's take her home," Van said, and together they lifted her up and carried her away.

Epilogue

It had been a week since the attack and attempted takeover of Fagan Pack territory. Since then, Cysure Corp had been taken over by members of the circle. Through their own investigating, it appeared that many documents and experimental cases had been destroyed or stolen. It sent both fear and awareness through the pack community and authorities that danger was still possible. They would continue to have men work on finding those who took the files and documents. Dani was more than ready to help, but her mates had other plans for her. They were discussing the future here and there because it usually turned into a fight of whether or not she could remain a detective and their fear of her being in constant danger.

She came up with the idea to help them and other wolves protect the circle of elders and the sanctity of the wolf community by being an investigator for their community crimes and offenses. They promised to think about it, but she knew her men. They were stubborn, they had tempers, and they were bossy pains in the ass.

Dani yelped as she felt the smack to her ass cheek as she lay cuddling in bed on her side.

Looking over her shoulder, she saw Van. There was some sort of commotion going on in the bathroom.

"Hey."

"Hey, yourself. Bossy pains in the ass, huh?" He knelt on the bed and leaned across her body, placing a hand on either side of her.

She smiled.

"You know you are," she teased.

He looked her body over, and it warmed from his gaze. They had all made love to her numerous times since that night she was abducted.

The sound of yelling from the bathroom drew her attention.

"What the hell are they doing in there?" she asked.

Van shook his head and chuckled. "Miele and Bently are filling up water guns. They brought a bunch of stuff for the pups at the BBQ we're going to. That's why you need to get up and get ready. There are important people to meet."

She smirked at him.

"Well, if my playful wolves hadn't kept me up all night, perhaps I wouldn't be so tired this morning."

He stroked her chin with his finger from her lips, down her neck, and across her nipples, which now felt hard and aroused.

"Someone wasn't complaining at all last night."

She felt her cheeks warm.

"What woman would complain as six sexy, hot men catered to her every sexual need and desire? You make no sense sometimes." She pulled back the covers and scooted under his arm to go use the bathroom.

She was naked but not insecure at all. Her men loved her body. They told her over and over again and showed her, too. Talk about a boost to her self-confidence. These men were her inspiration in life as well as her personal aphrodisiacs.

As she entered the bathroom, Bently and Miele were filling water guns. They stopped what they were doing to admire her and she smiled.

"Good morning. Can I please have the bathroom a few minutes?"

Bently kissed her on the cheek and caressed her breast. "Sure, sweetheart. You look really good."

She patted down her hair. "I probably look a mess."

"No, sweetheart, you look like a woman well loved by her men." Miele kissed her cheek while caressing her ass. Someway, somehow, even though her limbs ached and her body was tired, they aroused her, and she knew she could have sex with them any time and any way, because that is what they did to her.

"I can help you in the shower," Miele suggested.

"I'm good," she told them, and they smiled as they walked out.

* * * *

A few hours later, they sat around the picnic tables at a party that seemed utterly normal yet filled with both weres and humans. They played and talked and chatted about business, politics, and children growing up fast, just like normal people.

As she walked away from the small group of women, all wolves, who quietly chatted about their mates, she overheard a conversation between her men, the Fennigan Pack, and a few others.

"She's going to have to submit to our demands. I for one will not allow my woman to be so independent and work at that company with those men surrounding her, flirting with her, and trying to get into her pants," one wolf stated, and they all mumbled in agreement.

"I think we need to remind these women about the ways of pack wives. They are to be there for us first and foremost. That should keep them more than busy so they shouldn't need to work outside of the home," some other older guy stated.

She felt her blood boiling. She had met his and his brother's mate, and she was so sweet and very educated. She had a lot of great ideas for business.

"I can't believe what I'm hearing," their mate stated to Dani.

"I was eavesdropping myself." Dani saw two other women she'd met join them.

"What's going on?" one of them asked.

"The men are getting all ancient on us. My mates just basically stated that they want me barefoot, pregnant, and at their beck and call. They're jealous because other men find me attractive," she stated, annoyed.

"Insecure," one of the women added.

Dani looked behind them at the table filled with water guns. "I have an idea." They chuckled as she explained, and the other two women gathered two more women whose mates joined the group of men.

The women grabbed the water guns and slowly surrounded the men.

"Believe me, we understand your concerns. We're going through the same issues with our mate. She's quite independent," Bently stated.

"She sure is and she's got a temper, too," Miele added.

"We don't want her in danger. She's safest by our side," Van added.

"We all agree," Vanderlan said.

"That's the way it should be and has always been. Our mates need to take responsibility at home with the pack and not out in the world. They belong to us," one wolf stated.

"Well, we disagree," one of the women interrupted, and the men turned toward them.

Dani and all the women pointed the guns at the men.

"You need to wake up and get with the program." The one woman shot water straight at the wolf that last spoke.

The water gun fight began as the women shot and sprayed the men as the men searched for their own weapons.

Dani's ran out of water, and she ran toward the table with the guns, grabbing the largest one, a Super Soaker.

"Dani's got a gun!" Randolph yelled as he fired his own weapon.

The men, her men were shooting at her with small handguns because that was all that was left. Dani aimed and pressed her finger on the trigger, soaking the heck out of all her mates.

The place erupted in laughter, and Vanderlan snuck up behind Dani, disarming her before throwing her over his shoulder. The others followed.

Dani waved to the other women as their mates followed suit, tossing them over their shoulders and heading toward their vehicles.

She chuckled as the men dripped with water.

"Dani's got a gun? Nice warning, Randolph," Baher stated, annoyed as he squeezed out his T-shirt.

They got into the SUV and Vanderlan grabbed a fistful of Dani's T-shirt.

"You're in some serious trouble," he told her as Bently lifted her arms so Vanderlan could remove her shirt.

She shivered with anticipation as she looked toward the others, and Van began to drive home.

Vanderlan lifted her up and placed her on his lap. His hands smoothed up her thighs and under the skirt she wore.

"Payback's a bitch, mate." He covered her mouth with his own as he caressed her thighs and thrust up against her. She felt his cock through his wet pants. She felt so aroused and wild with need.

"Oh, you're not going to get fucked yet, mate. No, we have some plans for you," Baher stated firmly as Vanderlan released her lips. She felt roused, breathless.

"First we're going to take you home, strip you, then tie you to the bed," Bently informed her.

Baher unclipped her bra, removed it, then stroked her nipple, giving it a tug.

"Then we're going to spank that ass of yours," Van chimed in.

"I'm going to give that troublemaking mouth of yours a workout, baby, with my cock," Miele informed her, and she took a shaky breath, totally turned on by their words and their indications of what they planned on doing to her.

"You think so, huh?" she teased, and Vanderlan gripped her hips and thrust up against her needy pussy.

"Oh yeah, you're in for the ride of your life," Randolph told her as Van pulled into the driveway at the estate.

"Well, you asked for it, talking with those other wolves about controlling their mates and not allowing for independence or work outside of the home." The SUV stopped and the doors opened, everyone except for her and Vanderlan moved.

"You are our mate, and we would never deny you happiness. We're going to make you so aroused and needy and loved by us that you won't want to be away from us, never mind away from the bedroom." He scooted to the side and got out of the SUV, carrying a practically naked Dani toward the house.

She pressed her breasts against his chest as he carried her inside.

"You think you all are that good, huh?" she challenged. This was all a game, she felt their excitement and arousal and wanted them as much as they wanted her.

In a flash, he was up the stairs. Immediately she was stripped of her skirt and panties as the others removed their clothing, too.

Vanderlan passed her to Bently and Randolph, who laid her on the bed. They reached down near the bedposts and pulled restraining devices from the posts. The realization that they had always been there and at any time they could have pulled them out to restrain her made her aroused and excited.

"Those have been there?" she asked.

"Installed as soon as we found you and realized that you were our mate," Miele told her.

They attached the bindings. They were soft against her wrists, padded so no harm could come to her. In fact, she could easily slip out of them if need be.

"I feel like your prisoner," she whispered, hearing her own breath hitch with excitement as her naked, sexy men placed her body exactly how they wanted it.

She was sprawled out before them, naked and spread eagle as all six of them stood back with their arms crossed in front of their chests, admiring the view. Her pussy clenched with need.

She absorbed the sight of them—muscles, tattoos, and long, thick cocks ready to make love to their mate.

"Oh God, you're all so beautiful," she whispered, and they smiled.

"You're the beautiful one. But before we get started, there's something you should know."

"What?"

"We love the woman that you are, and as much as it would make us happier to keep you safe at home in our arms, we know how much your career means to you. We talked to our uncle. There is a position for you in the Special Investigations Unit. If you want it."

"Really?" she squealed. She loved them so much and they truly cared about making her happy. They accepted who she was and how hard she worked to achieve her professional position.

"But now it's punishment time," Van stated, and they were on her in a flash, licking, kissing, pinching, arousing every one of her senses until she was a coil wound so tight she was about to bust.

Van got between her legs. "You are ours for eternity, Daniella, and we shall cherish you every day of our lives."

She smiled wide as the tears filled her eyes.

She was in love with five wolves and a vampire. She didn't care about work, about a career, or about anything but having their love and being with them forever.

THE END

WWW.DIXIELYNNDWYER.COM

ABOUT THE AUTHOR

People seem to be more interested in my name than where I get my ideas for my stories from. So I might as well share the story behind my name with all my readers.

My momma was born and raised in New Orleans. At the age of twenty, she met and fell in love with an Irishman named Patrick Riley Dwyer. Needless to say, the family was a bit taken aback by this as they hoped she would marry a family friend. It was a modern-day arranged marriage kind of thing and my momma downright refused.

Being that my momma's families were descendents of the original English-speaking Southerners, they wanted the family bloodline to stay pure. They were wealthy, and my father's family was poor.

Despite attempts by my grandpapa to make Patrick leave and destroy the love between them, my parents married. They recently celebrated their sixtieth wedding anniversary.

I am one of six children born to Patrick and Lynn Dwyer. I am a combination of both Irish and a true Southern belle. With a name like Dixie Lynn Dwyer it's no wonder why people are curious about my name.

Just as my parents had a love story of their own, I grew up intrigued by the lifestyles of others. My imagination as well as my need to stray from the straight and narrow made me into the woman I am today.

For all titles by Dixie Lynn Dwyer, please visit
www.bookstrand.com/dixie-lynn-dwyer

Siren Publishing, Inc.
www.SirenPublishing.com

CPSIA information can be obtained at www.ICGtesting.com
Printed in the USA
BVOW03s1054100914

366266BV00033B/1075/P

9 781622 422852